THE
DIVINE
COMEDY

THE
DIVINE
COMEDY

Craig Raine

Atlantic Books
London

First published in Great Britain in 2012 by Atlantic Books,
an imprint of Atlantic Books Ltd.

1 2 3 4 5 6 7 8 9

A CIP catalogue record for this book is
available from the British Library.

ISBN: 9781848872837

Printed and bound by CPI Group (UK) Ltd, Croydon

Atlantic Books
An imprint of Atlantic Books Ltd
Ormond House
26–27 Boswell Street
London
WC1N 3JZ

www.atlantic-books.co.uk

– Hypocrite lecteur, – mon semblable, – mon frère!

– Baudelaire, 'Au lecteur'

After two minutes that felt like six minutes, Rysiek's electric toothbrush – a present from an English friend – had its brief but unmistakable orgasm. Normally, he never cleaned his teeth after lunch, but today he was going to see his dentist. Rysiek Harlan. You will be hearing more about him.

After two minutes that felt like six minutes.
The theme of subjectivity.

Its brief but unmistakable orgasm.
Precision. And, by contrast, the idea of human unreliability.

The machine, then, and the human being – the machine with God in the machine.

The dentist is important, too.

––––––

Adam came before Eve. Eve came after Adam. If this were not the case, the human race would die out. Imagine a world in which the woman turns away from her toiling partner because she has already come and she is feeling sleepy – and far too tired to wait for her mate to achieve his elusive orgasm. Eve has to come after Adam.

––––––

Once upon a time, there were three brothers (and a sister) who were Jewish. In fact, they were the children of the *mohel*. All three boys were circumcised, therefore. But the *mohel* was experienced and he knew from experience that, although circumcision was a religious and hygienic requirement, it could nevertheless entail certain disadvantages – the main one being the skin's loss of play along the shaft of the penis. Erect, the penis was solid, inflexible. Lose the prepuce in its entirety and you had a trombone without a slide. Masturbation was impossible without a lubricant. Well, not *impossible*, just rather awkward. *Good.* The *mohel* disapproved of the solitary vice.

Mutual heterosexual masturbation was also awkward. *Not good.* The wife's pleasuring of the husband prior to full intercourse held (the *mot juste*) two possibilities. The first was unlubricated manhandling. With the hope, perhaps, that, were the wife naturally inventive or sexually savvy, saliva might stimulate the secretion of prostatic fluid (known in German as *der Sehnsuchtstropfen*, the drop of longing).

(Strike out 'sexually savvy': the *mohel* harboured no such 'hope'. His wife was an autodidact. His sons' wives should also be inexperienced – ignorant yet intuitive.)

The second possibility was that, without the wife's spit, the man would be sufficiently excited to secrete his own transparent lubricant – the sufficient excitement creating possibly unbearable excitement, in which teleology would inevitably and rapidly overcome the desire not to come.

(There was a third possibility. But the *mohel* did not allow the idea of fellatio to leave his mind. He could not stop it entering.)

So the *mohel* circumcised his male children subtly, modestly, semi-symbolically. He practised circumcision as synecdoche, the part for the whole. The entire glans was not revealed – only the tip with its goldfish mouth.

The penis in its polo neck.

With the result, in the case of the eldest boy, of the operation being re-performed – at the age of seven, in hospital, under local anaesthetic – to detach the prepuce from the glans, where it was joined in two places. An unforeseen eventuality, that attachment, preventing the play of skin.

In case, therefore, the foreskin should re-attach itself after separation, it was completely removed. Preventing the play of skin.

In his mid-twenties the same boy had a cyst removed from just below his exposed glans. The black-edged crater healed and almost vanished, as the surgeon had promised.

The second son of the *mohel* discovered a lump on his right testicle at the age of fifteen. The female doctor conducted a manual examination and sent the boy for ultrasound inspection. The lump was diagnosed as a non-malignant, epididymal cyst. Surgery was not required or recommended.

The third and youngest son of the *mohel* was discovered to have an undescended testicle at birth. The prognosis was that, except exceptionally, the testicle would descend of its own accord at some later stage. However, the latest Swedish research had demonstrated a correlation – purely statistical, not physiological – between the onset of testicular cancer in males in their mid-twenties and the occurrence of an undescended testicle at birth. It was decided, therefore, to operate – to induce the descent surgically, severing the testicle from its future phantom Siamese twin, the diseased and late-descending statisticle.

As the *mohel* discussed the matter with the medics and his wife, he recalled a monorchid cousin whose testicular cancer forced him to leave the Royal Navy and the royal yacht *Britannia*. These troublesome testicles.

The *mohel's* daughter had none of these problems. Her problems would come later – after childbirth had weakened her pelvic floor, leaving her with a slight disposition to incontinence and a tendency to prolapse of the uterus. And haemorrhoids. Of course. Naturally.

The divine comedy.

On the ceiling of the delivery suite, a haze of blood.

The shaven vagina is now no longer shaved – unless there is to be a caesarean. The enema is no longer obligatory. A little shit is no longer shocking.

The vaginal sweep is when the midwife inserts her anointed rubber glove to enlarge the dilating cervix. You can see the play of muscles on her forearm. When the hand is withdrawn, a spate of jelly and cream is released.

Birth via the vaginal canal is possible when the cervix is eight centimetres dilated. When fully dilated it is ten centimetres.

An episiotomy is a cut made on the entrance walls of the vagina to expedite the birth and to prevent tearing. Tearing is harder to repair than a clean cut. The outer lips of the vagina and the perineum are injected with local anaesthetic. A pair of blunt-ended scissors is worked past the baby's head. Making the cut isn't easy. It takes two hands and strength.

The anus is on a stalk like a head of broccoli. The midwife cuts a modesty pad from a sanitary towel to shield it from the student midwives watching. Birth depends on the action of excretion.

The child is a little channel swimmer, covered in vernix, shivering, with goggles of flesh over the eyes. The colour purple. Which changes to crimson when it cries.

When they clip and cut the umbilical cord, you can hear the scissors going through grit.

To stitch the cut, they put your legs in stirrups. The blood is swabbed with frothing jaundiced antiseptic. The surgeon counts the layers of epidermis, dermis, hypodermis briskly like a bank teller and orders them tidily. The needle comes threaded from the sterilised pack and is held in a pair of plier-ended scissors. Each stitch is pulled to a peak, a little white pimple, before going on to the next.

You can feel the scar for six months. Like a needle left behind. I've got you under my skin.

The process isn't painless. The endorphins released by the body are inadequate. The epidural works – but carries a risk, if only a slight one, statistically.

The process is a miracle.

———

The four-week-old baby boy was naked in the health visitor's scales, bawling but doing well, having made up his birth weight and gone beyond it. A crimson cry, he squirmed and raged from lusty lungs.

The visitor leaned in and looked over her glasses to see the calibrated dial, then noted the new weight, first in pencil on her clipboard, then in the baby's notes. She was Brobdingnagian in the pelvis, swathed in a bolt of boldly patterned houndstooth tweed. Turning to the mother, she said, 'He's blessed.'

'I'm sorry?' the mother responded.

'He's blessed.' She was looking at the baby's penis and invited the mother to follow her glance.

The mother's expression gave nothing away. She was puzzled and was halfway home before she realised that the health visitor was referring to the size of the baby's penis.

In two weeks' time the parents had an appointment with the plastic surgeon to decide about the baby's hypospadias – first degree, so relatively minor, a urethral misalignment easily repaired or possibly left well alone. 'Provided he can urinate standing up ...' the doctor shrugged.

So, a mixed blessing.

(But not, thank God for small mercies, penoscrotal transposition. Think about it.)

The female consultant plastic surgeon inspected the same baby's foreskin, fissured at the frenum, and pronounced it, through chocolate-red lipstick, to be perfectly functional. Erection and intercourse would be unimpaired. A repair would be 'only cosmetic'.

Only cosmetic?

Three-quarters of every chemist's shop is given over to Max Factor, Rimmel, Bourjois, Elizabeth Arden, Neutrogena,

Garnier, L'Oréal, Dior, Chanel … The cosmetic industry has a turnover of billions of pounds – a figure that demonstrates the unimportance to everyone of the cosmetic.

In the *Independent* newspaper (8 May 2009) the television critic Alice-Azania Jarvis reviewed a Channel 4 programme about male bodies, *Extreme Male Beauty*. She began by deploring 'physical fascism' that mocked physical flaws – like 'moobs', which are 'male boobs'. Then she mocked male efforts to improve their bodies. She concluded: 'Next week: penises. Might give that a miss.' Penis ennui. When Jacques Derrida was asked what he would like to ask the great philosophers of the past – Kant, Hegel, Heidegger – he said he would like to know about their sex lives. He stipulated that he didn't want a porno movie version but rather a sense of what this occluded yet central part of their lives was actually like. I am not sure I believe in penis ennui any more than I believe in penis envy. But curiosity definitely exists. When Derrida came to Oxford to give an Amnesty lecture at the Sheldonian in February 1992, a Jewish undergraduate called Tommy Karshan told me he happened to be standing at the urinal next to Derrida's. He looked.

As a matter of fact, Alice-Azania Jarvis looked, too, despite her advertised impatience, at the next episode of *Extreme Male Beauty*. But then, turned off, she turned off.

Blake's 'The Book of Thel' touches on the black laughter attendant on the physical:

7

'Why a tender curb upon the youthful burning boy?
'Why a little curtain of flesh on the bed of our desire?'

Meaning, of course, the foreskin and the hymen, potential obstacles both – the second obvious enough, the first less obvious, until you recall that Gerard Manley Hopkins was operated on at the late age of 29 for a troublesome prepuce. Blake is generalising, perhaps from personal knowledge. But there is nothing in principle that he needs to retract.

———

The morning after the widow's party, the phone rang twice while she was still having breakfast. All-Bran Pétales and skimmed milk. It was 7 a.m. She had been up for an hour, had showered and watered her plants. Neither caller apologised for ringing this early. They were old, so it wasn't early.

The first caller was Richard. He wanted the address in Versailles of that sexy blonde 52-year-old he'd met at the widow's party. Yes, *mon Dieu*, he liked her. Yes, he would follow it up. Let me just get a something to write with. Absolutely. Thank you. Yes. Thank you. Bye.

Richard was 70 and twice-divorced. His hands shook a little, but he still had his hair.

The second caller was Larissa, a Russian émigré, who was 61. She talked for an hour because, after the party, she had lost her virginity to a 68-year-old. He had just left her apartment. She was excited.

'You know, I didn't orgasm. But it didn't matter. You know, I didn't expect to. And it is so nice being kissed. His breath smelled a little, but it didn't matter. At his age, you expect it. You do. I was shy, you know, of taking off my clothes. I have

8

this appendix scar and that thing on my knee. I must get it removed. But he wasn't so great either, you know. Little bit fat. Not gross. Just a little bit, you know, drawn with a wobbly pencil. One with a broken point so you can't put any pressure. And his thing was fine. Big. But the balls make me laugh, you know. So funny. No one tells you how funny they are. He wants me to put his thing in my mouth. Like a whistle. He says, will I blow it. Is that? Did you ever do that? Oh, OK. I just didn't know, you know. Well, he changed his mind and jiggled his thing for a bit before he put it inside me. Didn't hurt a bit. A *very* nice feeling, as a matter of fact. Iris, is there always that smell? Is that? Oh, it is. OK. I am so excited, I can't tell you. I am really in love.'

That evening, the sexy blonde 52-year-old was preparing dinner for her guests when the door bell rang. It was Richard, the 70-year-old, asking to come in. She pecked him on the cheek, explained she was expecting guests, asked if he would join them, and gave him a couple of scotch bonnet chillis to chop. After fifteen minutes he needed the toilet. She pointed to the one in the downstairs hall. Three minutes later he was out on the hall tiles, demanding the bathroom and taking the stairs two at a time.

She could hear the taps thundering into her tub as he saw to his burning bush and its scorched environs.

By Jove. *Mon Dieu.*

He left without saying goodbye.

Circumcision: a hygienic measure with religious and racial overtones. But basically a question of cleanliness. However, as

9

we know, the physical quickly acquires moral implications. Cleanliness is next to godliness – for example.

Which is why, thirty years ago, the brother of a friend got himself circumcised before his wedding by way of cleansing his cock of a previous girl. Sore at himself, he made himself sore. A fresh smart.

Funny thing, foreskin. 'Which an age of prudence can never retract.' Apparently. In this case.

Funny thing, humour.

(You say Jehovah and I can't say YHWH. Let's cut the whole thing off.)

————

This is a story of circumcision.

This is a story of circumcision and slaughter.

In which the Lord God of Israel ransacks and pillages, piles up the prepuces and enjoys His own joke.

Dinah, the daughter of Jacob by his first wife, Leah, was secretly in love with a Hivite prince, Shechem. When he laughed, his teeth were strong and white. His torso was a hairless, tanned bronze. His nipples were darker, lustrous, cupreous. He was clean-shaven with a wide flattish straight nose and fine lips at once sensual and geometric. He was the opposite of her scraggly bearded Jewish brothers, whose chests were scribbled over with pubic hair. Shechem's blue-veined forearms and his lovely long fingers shamed the stubby, hairy hands of her sibs, Simeon and Levi. She loved everything about him – but especially his uncircumcised cock.

10

Then Dinah's period was late. Shechem gently thumbed away her tears and spoke tenderly to her. 'I will take the blame. Behold my strategy. You will say I have defiled you against your will in the orchard by night. Then I will offer to undo the misdeed and the shame by taking your hand. By this means, our marriage – until now a dream and an impossibility – will be countenanced by your tight-knit tribe who otherwise have set their face against all thought of exogamy.'

So Dinah tore her robe, scooped up the dust, and let it trickle on her hair and garments. Breaking one sandal strap, she ran, limping, to the tents of her tribe. She decided not to weep, preferring the authority of silence and secrecy. It took her father Jacob some time before he discovered exactly how his daughter was defiled. She sat cross-legged, staring at the line of the horizon, answering his concern with curt monosyllables.

No, she did not know his name.

She did not think he was a Jew.

Why not?

He wasn't hairy.

But I am a smooth man, unlike my brother Esau, Jacob objected.

Dinah wanted to point out that, while Esau had a hairy nose and upper cheeks and back, in reality Jacob wasn't the depilated patriarch of reputation. She refrained, however, and looked at her dirtied hands for an answer instead.

Well?

His penis …

You saw his penis?

She refused to answer for shame.

In the dark?

Now she could see an answer was swiftly needed.

He made me … In my mouth. Before … And it was different.

From what you expected?

Yes.

By now her brothers and their brothers' brothers were returning from the fields and the evening air was thick with threats against the Philistines.

As the clamour rose, Prince Shechem and his father, King Hamar, headed a torchlit progress up the hill. A Hivite soldier beat a melancholy drum. The delegation stood at a little distance in the twilight and Hamar addressed the Jewish patriarch.

Son of Isaac.

Grandson of Abraham.

It shames me greatly that this our royal son (he held up a torch to Shechem's superb profile) has permitted passion to overrule a lifetime of daily discretion. We feel your anger and the threat to the fragile peace between our tribes. Instead of war, instead of blood, we propose alliance. Prince Shechem desires her hand in marriage, with a bride-price well above the current market levels, by way of reparation.

Simeon and Levi shouted then that they would never let their sister marry out.

But Jacob counselled quiet and consideration of the Hivite king's proposals.

Further – Hamar shouted – let there be general intermarriage between our two tribes. Here the land is plentiful enough for all. And you are welcome to join your tents to our tents. What say you?

Jacob held his peace. No one could see his visage or read the expression there. He was aware that in a war, their forces would not be equal. However belligerent he felt, something shrewder than force was required. He feared the Canaanites and also the Perizzites – and, most of all, inglorious isolation.

Then Simeon, Dinah's elder brother, shouted across the broken ground between the sides that it was an insult to expect Jewish women to go with the uncircumcised outsiders. Even were the women willing, it was impossible to countenance.

Jacob cleared his throat mildly. God had come to his aid. When everyone was silent, listening, he said in a low, carrying voice, replete with authority and experience – But if the uncircumcised were circumcised …

The tribe of Jacob took in the breadth of vision, the boldness of the strategy, without knowing quite what lay behind it. There was the sense of a master-diplomatist making his crucial move, a move whose ramifications were as yet concealed. They didn't like it, they couldn't see it, but they acquiesced.

And so the Hivites were circumcised, every man in that walled city, every man that left or entered by the southern or the northern gate.

On the third day, when they were sore, Simeon and Levi entered the city by night and dragged their hysterical sister home, having slain Shechem as he reposed, bandaged, on his malachite couch. And King Hamar likewise. And every awkward, disadvantaged, unsuspecting male.

The tribe of Jacob seized the flocks, the herds, the donkeys, the supercilious camels, the wealth, the wives, their little ones.

And Jacob disapproved. Too late. He was angry against the anger of his sons. But not displeased.

It was the smiting of the circumcised uncircumcised – he was a man of God and as a man of peace his alibi was still intact.

(Who put the laughter in slaughter?)

Nothing anti-Semitic there. Unless the Bible is anti-Semitic. Which, come to think of it, it often is. More or less every time the Israelites misbehave. The chosen people? Or the picked-on people? And anyway, my version of Genesis 33 doesn't follow God's word to the letter. It takes liberties, freedoms with the narrative emphases. Oh God, God, it isn't meant to be anti-Semitic.

Since T. S. Eliot, everyone needs to be careful.

If the Bible can be anti-Semitic, it must be possible to be a Jew and also anti-Semitic. In the *New York Review of Books* (17 July 2008) Zadie Smith considered the idea of Kafka as a self-hating, anti-Semitic Jew – and digitally adjusted the posture until Kafka became only a writer incapable of any group identity, whether national or racial.

A French secular Jew wrote a second novel that was turned down by two American publishing houses because they thought it was anti-Semitic. He could suddenly see himself as a reviled figure, a disagreeable novelist. Not Céline, perhaps, but Michel Houellebecq. Controversial. Whereas he wanted to be an acclaimed and popular novelist. Like Zadie Smith.

His first novel, *Jacobin*, hadn't been translated into English, so this second novel, *Délice*, was his first big chance in the US and international market.

When he flew to the United States, therefore, he took precautions. He cut his fringe back to the hairline and grew semi-sidelocks so that he looked subtly reminiscent of a yeshiva boy. He wore white shirts with the shirt-tail fashionably half out – fashionably and Jewishly.

Is it anti-Semitic to say that, normally, with the fringe, he looked like a young handsome version of Hitler – without the moustache? Same nose. Same charm.

As it happened, the book never happened. *Délice* wasn't reviewed. So it didn't matter at all.

––––––––

Rex had gone to bed with his future father-in-law.

The night before, they had thrown a party and several guests had stayed over, so all the sleeping arrangements had been improvised at 3 in the morning. Girls sleeping four to a double bed, boys on the floor of the sitting room and Rex in bed with his future father-in-law – a six-foot-tall 54-year-old ex-wrestler wearing only a large pair of Wolsey X fronts. On his shoulders, silver epaulettes of hair. The Omega wristwatch was partially overgrown. The rising register of his snores snagged and slurred.

The bedroom curtains were unlined and thin. By six o'clock, when Rex woke to find his fiancée beside him, the pinkish light was faint but clear. She had come to him with her hair up. He could see the black sequin of the mole on her cheek, a perfect circle. Her eyes were closed. The lids were oiled. Three

15

tiny sparks of mascara lodged in her eyelashes. One eyebrow was mussed. The other fluently flowed to vanishing point. Her lips were slightly parted. On the line of her upper lip he could see one very small blackhead where the pink pigment joined her paler skin. The pores of her skin were pricked clean. A vein on her neck flexed and flexed again.

He moved on to her body. As his hand reached the waistband of her knickers and began to ease them off, her eyes opened, changed from brown to grey and watched him with incredulity. 'Shhh,' he said, 'it's OK, it's OK.' Then her whole face morphed and became her father's face.

Rex thrashed and babbled and pretended to sleep – wide awake and shaken by the helicopter of his heart.

———

Parking was tight in the marina, so Johnny, the racing driver, took over – nudging and chivvying while Rex watched the front wheels swivel and breakdance and made sure the car in front wasn't rammed. He held his hands apart: 'You've got six inches.'

Johnny leaned his head out of the window, wittily, pithily: 'I should be so lucky.'

———

'Show me a man who has not measured his penis – and I will show you a liar' – Icelandic proverb

———

Or an ostrich.

With plumes like soundless surf. With tough three-toed claws. With a sore, scrotal, not quite hairless head. Out of sight. Up to its neck.

If you don't want to know the score, look away now.

———

In the *Radio Times* (22–8 April 2000) Andrew Duncan interviewed Eddie Irvine, the Formula One (F1) Grand Prix (GP) racing driver, the year after Irvine came second to Mika Häkkinen in the World Championship *by one point, in the last race*. These infinitesimal differences which matter so much. Not to mention the sly comedy of those abbreviations ...

Duncan was candid about Irvine's limitations as a human being – boring and boastful and one of the boys. Duncan reminded Irvine of the Channel Four (C4) documentary *The Inside Track* – which had footage of Irvine leaving the shower with the words, 'Did you get my big knob?'

Irvine explained the joke: 'If I did have a big one, which I don't, it wouldn't have been funny.'

In fact, the documentary, which I saw (by accident), includes footage of a girl at a party saying that Irvine doesn't have a big cock. Or that he's modestly endowed. Or small. I forget the exact words. Culpably, because these judgements are by no means the same. Not at all. *Tiny*, for instance. But I distinctly remember she didn't seem fussed. Certainly not as fussed as the documentary makers or the *Radio Times* interviewer.

Liz Winter, an editor at *The Times Literary Supplement*, told Timothy Garton Ash, the political journalist, historian and fellow member of the European Classics Trust, that when she was a young student of Russian she had slept with Joseph Brodsky, in Leningrad, and that he was 'very small and circumcised'. An even lower score than Eddie Irvine. But Brodsky was persistent and successful, a serial Don Juan. This is well known. While recognising a 'Petrarchan' side to Brodsky, even the discreet Seamus Heaney doesn't seriously challenge his interviewer in *Stepping Stones* (2008) when Dennis O'Driscoll says, '*Brodsky was reportedly an unreconstructed macho male.*' I believe that his almost undentable self-confidence extended to his cock – the feel-good factor, an area of solipsism where the force of desire is all important.

We experience hardness subjectively as augmented dimension – in addition to the objective augmented dimension of the erection. This hypothesis is easy to test. You have an unwanted erection. It doesn't seem small. Especially if it won't diminish. And the Queen is approaching.

Robert Lowell has a poem in *Notebook* about Oskar Kokoschka. Kokoschka told him that Renoir said he painted with his penis. Just as well that writers write with their brains. In Dorothy Farnan's *Auden in Love*, there is a missing footnote. When I read the Simon and Schuster typescript for Fabers, there was a footnote giving the precise dimensions of Auden's penis. I said it should be dropped. And it was dropped, though probably not at my request. I mentioned the footnote to Charles Monteith, my predecessor as Poetry Editor. He told me that Wystan was a tremendous bore about the small bore of his cock and deeply envious of Chester Kallman's genital bounty. I have forgotten the precise figures volunteered by the excised footnote. 4½ inches perhaps. Or 3½ inches. But was that 3½ inches floppy? Or 3½ inches stiffy? 3½ inches floppy would be more than OK.

By the way, these 'digressions' are not digressions. They are not by the way.

———

Even at the age of 29, Julia's hair was barcoded. Now, at 62, it was a solid helmet of bright pewter, level with her lean, brown jawbone. As she looked at her wedding ring, she could observe the bold play of tendons on the back of her tanned thin hands. The student doctor was telling her she had cancer. Of the bone marrow.

He had found her reading her notes – left on the desk by the consultant – and assumed that she knew the diagnosis. Perhaps he thought her doctorate in zoology was a doctorate in medicine. He wanted to be nice. 'Myeloma. Broad term, actually. In your case,' he gestured at the crisp yellow folder on which her hands were resting, 'it's serious – well, it's always serious – but not hopeless.'

His fingernails were clean and cut short. She liked that.

And he wasn't entirely wrong about her medical knowledge. After the initial tests, she'd done some reading and asked various medical friends a few questions. She'd looked on the web. So she had a shrewd and accurate idea of her chances immediately – two to five years or the possibility of stabilising the condition for a longer, indeterminate period. She might reach 70 with luck. Longer if she were luckier.

When the consultant, Aaronovitch, proposed that he should take her into his confidence, she pretended complete ignorance – to protect the student doctor and to hear the fullest possible account of her illness. Aaronovitch's diagnosis differed from the student doctor's in no significant particular.

'I should tell you, Mr Aaronovitch,' Julia said, 'what you couldn't possibly know unless you've got my GP's notes from way back, that my blood count has always been very low. I mean before all this. When I was well. So I'd say that I may be less ill than I look. On paper. So to speak.'

Her acute hearing picked up the sound of his hairy hand palpating his chin. The sound of static. To tell Julia he was thinking. Considering. Weighing. Being judicious. Finally, he folded his arms across his waistcoat, leaned back in his chair, inclined his head a little, looked directly into Julia's eyes – and proposed the experimental treatment he had been contemplating for six months before the onset of the symptoms which had brought her to his hospital.

'In *that* case,' he said, 'blood to make up the count and chemo. One pill a month. That's all. New thing. Massively powerful, of course. But definitely worth a try. Might just do the trick.' He reached and clicked his Montblanc rollerball twice.

They looked each other in the eye.

'They sent for some doctors | In sneezles | And wheezles,' Julia said gravely. 'To tell them what ought | To be done.'

Mr Aaronovitch lifted a quizzical eyebrow.

'All sorts and conditions | Of famous physicians | Came hurrying round | At a run,' Julia answered, without smiling. 'You're the expert, that's all.'

The medication had a very beautiful name. Mandragorax. By a pharmaceutical company which knew its Shakespeare.

In six months it had completely stripped the nerves of her hands. She could feel nothing.

What is God? This is one of the great questions to which there is no certain answer. And the other is, what is the size of your penis? It depends.

Sometimes it depends more. Sometimes it depends less. It varies. But Heisenberg has told us that our involvement in the experiment means precise measurement is impossible. Or should that be Schrödinger, whose cat is both living and dead until the observer observes. The interference of the observer is especially true of psychic measurement. There are good days and there are bad days. Adolescents, fortunately, are semi-erect and so never have to face up to their smallest manifestations, except in the sea – the sea which is not only scrotumtightening, but also penisshrinking.

The sea, of course, is not alone in this genital specialisation. Fear is another expert in downsizing. As a war correspondent for the US State Department, John Steinbeck took part in the assault on Isola di Ventotene, an island off the coast of Italy, north of Naples. Douglas Fairbanks Jr was the officer in charge. Steinbeck was brave enough to admit he was afraid on these missions. The degree of fear was made manifest when, before the landing, he went to the heads for a piss and couldn't find his penis because it had retracted so thoroughly, so cravenly, so sensibly. Or it may have been Robert Capa who tells this story about himself in *Slightly Out of Focus*.

Whether the penis depends more – or less – sometimes depends on who is telling the story.

In *A Good Read* (Radio 4, 21 April 2002), Rosie Boycott, Jackie Kay and Frank Delaney discussed Hemingway's *Across the River and into the Trees*. Delaney praised Hemingway's spare style but said he'd asked Martha (Irishly pronounced *Marta*) Gelhorn, Hemingway's ex-wife, how he'd arrived at this style. 'The old bastard had a very small vocabulary,' she replied. Rosie Boycott: 'I knew her well, too, and that wasn't the only thing that was small, according to her.'

Here is an interesting footnote to Rosie Boycott's innuendo. In the *New Yorker* (31 October 2005), George Packer was reviewing Stephen Koch's *The Breaking Point: Hemingway, Dos Passos, and the Murder of José Robles*. The review contains this passage about Hemingway and Martha Gelhorn: 'he [Hemingway] also fell in love with Gelhorn … In Madrid, he offered literary advice and patronage; she educated him in Popular Front propaganda while accommodating him sexually to the extent, according to one biographer, of undergoing a widening procedure known as vaginoplasty.' Which tells a different story. A whole new dimension.

———

With the failure of Mandragorax to do anything – except damage Julia – Mr Aaronovitch adopted more conventional treatment – a gradualist chemotherapy, administered by ID and closely monitored in the hospital over half a day and a night. Julia endured nausea and massive temperature fluctuations – her green hospital shift black with sweat and vacuum-packed against her scalded body. But no hair loss.

She began to stabilise. She played tennis. She swam.

Here she is, her skin the reddish-brown of bresaola, trapping tennis balls between racket and foot, crooking her knee, patting the plush. Here is the sweat-shadow left by her hand on the red leather racket handle. So tanned that her eyelids are pale if – *pain* – she closes her eyes. Here she is bald – lifting the squeaky flap of her white rubber bathing hat to tuck out of sight strands of her livid hair. Folds, a cape of chlorinated water gather at her neck as she strokes down the pool in little pulses, touches with two hands together and turns in an eddy. She is a burglar in her black goggles and striped bathing costume. In the changing room she hooks a finger under the rubber helmet and shakes her hair free. Bright grey, damp at the tips.

Mr Aaronovitch was surprised by her comparative recovery, that her immune system was still operational and effective, given its virtual extinction a few months previously. He persuaded Julia to take part in another experiment. His argument was calculated to appeal to her scientific instinct. Though unlikely to succeed in the short term, the new treatment might be valuable in the long term. Julia's proven powers of recuperation suggested to Aaronovitch that this new course of chemo, though carrying a significant risk, was unlikely to be fatal. However, its development, the necessary crucial refinements, depended on the use of a human guinea pig.

Julia thought of her beloved lab rats – the healthy and sleekit, the medicated and ungainly, carrying their single tumours like Quasimodo, their double tumours like Bactrians. And she signed the contract with Mr Aaronovitch's Montblanc rollerball. *Click-ick.* The contract promised not to withhold antibiotics.

In the event they were withheld. 'If you could just hang in there a little bit longer, Julia.' Mr Aaronovitch had stopped calling her Dr Duddington when she stopped being his patient and became, as it were, a colleague on the signing of the contract.

Here she is in her shift – too tired to tie the tell-tails behind her. Her buttocks have vanished. You can see her coccyx. There is hair all over her body. She can hardly make her jaws move to eat. Her throat is so ulcerated that swallowing is impossible. An amber mosaic. Her tongue is black-indigo. She cannot keep food down.

Talking is difficult. So many movements required that it takes her ten minutes, with rests between every whispered word, to say the first line of 'They all made a note / Of the state of her throat.' It is so painful for Julia that Byron, her husband, tries to complete the second line as soon as he recognises the quotation. But he fails at the pronoun – *his? her?*– and is so upset he has to leave the room.

When Mr Aaronovitch agreed at last to the suspension of treatment and the resumption of antibiotics, she was unable to take them orally. Byron had to push the suppositories up her rectum, taking gobs and shreds of flesh with them.

She bled from her vagina and rectum and, as she declined, began to soil herself. At the end, she was very weak and found it hard to walk. Byron took her upstairs, holding her thin hands. Her face was very pale, so pale she looked as if she were wearing lipstick.

He said: 'You're very weak. You're finding it hard to walk.'

She smiled and water came out of her mouth and she died in his arms.

———

After the undertaker had been, Byron kissed her and realised how dead she was. She had gone. She wasn't there. But he couldn't put the lid on the coffin. After three days the moulded symmetrical smile began to pull to one side. It began to look more like a smirk. He wondered if he should turn off the central heating all over the house, not just in the spare room.

Byron was unable to sleep and sat in her study in the kneeling chair, working his way through the diaries she kept in the beige filing cabinet. They recorded his bad behaviour during their twenty-year marriage. Where were the tender moments? Unrecorded. He read on, compelled, remorseful, weeping, nodding off now and then, only to be woken by his own sobs. 'B impossible. Drunk Encaenia garden party. Told principal everyone bisexl. Sodomised at Central School S & D: enjoyed it. Explained proximity of prostate to rectum wall accounts for male pleasure. Only drawback loose stools next morning. But that wd apply to wm also. In car I sd: B why do you do this? *What? What do I do?* Make things up. You're like a kid. Anything to be centre of attentn. *Fuck off. Rather be fucked up arse by poofter than service you.*'

All his jealousies, all his tantrums, all his sulks, were there in the diaries, written up like experiments, in Julia's methodical notation. And only Byron knew that these episodes were oblique expressions of his love for her. They had no children. She was 40 when they married and committed to her career. Sometimes she joked that she had a daughter called Trilobites. So children were out of the question – which suited him fine – but he got into the habit of creating a scene whenever he felt her concentration falter, flicker, unfocus. Byron wanted her attention undivided.

He succeeded. 'Dread B's rants. Think about them all time. Back of my mind all time. Hates me. Why?' He found no expressions of love.

'I stripped the nerves of her heart,' he would say in the street to any of their mutual friends. 'I was the chemo before the chemo. So domineering, so rude, so impossible. Christ, you should read her diaries. You find out. You think, she *knows* I care. But you find out she doesn't. She doesn't know. I tortured her.'

And he would stand there crying even after the friend had escaped. He didn't burst into tears. He was already in tears as soon as he saw anyone who had known her. 'I never learn. I never fucking learn, do I? Even the funeral. Even that. I made all the guests go in the Land Rover. And I made a fucking scene. I was embarrassing.'

They had taken all of Julia's field trips together in the Land Rover. At the graveside there was a freak summer hailstorm. Byron's black tie was pasted to his shirt. His face was so wet you couldn't tell how hard he was crying. He took out a copy (with worn corners) of *Now We Are Six* and tried to read 'Us Two'. The first stanza was a fight for control, looking away from the wet page, lips parted and dripping. The hailstones thrashed and popped. Where the clay began the earth looked like tiger stone. Then everything seemed to speed up, until the final stanza – which took a lifetime because Byron's mouth became suddenly difficult and stiff.

> *So wherever I am, there's always Pooh,*
> *There's always Pooh and Me.*
> *'What would I do?' I said to Pooh,*
> *'If it wasn't for you,' and Pooh said: 'True,*
> *It isn't much fun for One, but Two*
> *Can stick togeth …*

The slewed mouth of a stroke victim.

Byron flung himself on the wet coffin, which slipped out of his embrace and dropped a wreath of chrysanthemums. He fell. One knee was muddied and somehow his nose began to bleed.

For two years he was a grief automat, crying unstoppably at the mention of her name. Then he remarried – a younger woman – and was a difficult husband.

———

On 22 June 2001 two poet-editors recorded a radio programme for the BBC called *Fine Lines*, presented by Christopher Cook. One guest poet was Michael Schmidt, the publisher of Carcanet Books and the editor of *P N Review*. They had to read about four poems each and talk about editing magazines.

One of Schmidt's choices was his poem 'Sisera', a phrase of which the other poet had praised when reviewing *A Change of Affairs* in the *New Statesman* in 1978. The poem is voiced for Sisera, the Canaanite general, killed by Jael, who drives a spike through his head. In this version Sisera goes on – living but traumatised, lying low in his tent.

The other poet asked Michael Schmidt if he would like to explain the manifest but occluded subtext of his poem. He answered like Bartleby. The other poet suggested that the subtext was sexual fear. Schmidt agreed, but would not elaborate.

The extraordinary usefulness of the historical mask, like Piotr's poem 'Peter the Great to His Courtesan'. But you need to know a few things about Piotr.

———

Piotr was 42, married to Basia, the father of three sons, a professor of English at the Instytut Anglistyki in the University of Krakow. Three things worried him.

First, he was having an affair with Agnieszka, the poetess, who wore spectacles and looked like Nana Mouskouri.

Second, he had recently undergone a series of tests to establish if he had inherited the predisposition of his family to die of cancer in their late forties, as his mother had done.

And, third, his blond eyebrows, always strongly marked, had gone Nietzschean almost overnight. They were the family eyebrows, his father's eyebrows – two intense pelts half an inch high which made him look middle aged. His elder brother, Czesław, the architect, had an identical pair, but he was 50.

There was to be a fourth thing, but as yet he knew nothing of it.

The affair with Agnieszka bothered him not because he felt guilty about Basia, his wife – though he did feel guilty – but because Agnieszka's poetry was notorious for its candour and explicitness. Every year produced a new 48-page volume in which the slimness was inversely proportionate to the indiscretion. Piotr wrote poetry himself, less prolifically and more guardedly. He had written poems about his affair with Agnieszka but his way with pathetic fallacy meant that even Basia could read them without guessing their true provenance. The nearest he had come to confessional poetry was a dramatic monologue entitled 'Peter the Great to His Courtesan' – where the Czar forbade his mistress to 'rust his sword' and issued other majestically obscure imperatives.

Agnieszka's poetry, though, had her taking off her horn-rims to kiss her lover in the Kool Kats Jazz Club or giving a blow-job on the back seat of the bus to Nowa Huta. And her titles were nearly always dates and places.

One day he expected to read a poem about his eyebrows. (In fact, the poem responsible for all the damage was about quite another physical feature.) Or a poem with his phone number or his address in the title, ul. Sienkiewicza 35 m. 5. Particularly since his apartment was often the easiest place for the lovers to meet – as they were going to meet on this rainy day in June. He taught classes in the mornings but in the afternoon his students had exams. Agnieszka walked from the nearby Film School, where she worked in the cataloguing department. His sons would be in school till 4 and Basia's job with a foreign press agency meant that, because of the time difference, she was never home before six o'clock.

As soon as Agnieszka arrived, Piotr put the chain on the door and the pair undressed quickly and silently on opposite sides of the sofa bed. Like a married couple in a cold room. But the thick curve of his erection was ready before they even touched. He could smell her genitals across the tartan blanket – the blanket with tell-tail tassels she always brought in her tote bag.

She took off her spectacles.

On the sofa bed, she seldom repeated herself. This particular afternoon, as her features warped with pleasure, Piotr heard her agonised whisper, 'I want to, aah, suck a dog's ridgy, aah, sharp little cock.' And he came, too.

Afterwards, they talked, invariably about the same thing – Piotr's post-coital desire to end the affair and Agnieszka's passionate opposition. 'We are like mayflies. We live only for an afternoon and we must take whatever joy is given us.' This was the argument she always urged.

Piotr thought of the tests he had undergone – the barium meals, the endoscopies, the soreness of his throat after tubes had been pushed down it, the yellow bruise in the crook of his arm where blood had been taken. But there was also something comic in her chosen image for man's transience – the indestructible trope of the doomed mayfly. And he thought of the character in Chekhov's *Ivanov* who says that mankind is like a flower in a field. Along comes a goat – no more flower. The ear-pieces of Agnieszka's spectacles, he noticed, were arranged around a bottle of Basia's scent, brought back from England by her sister. *Je Reviens.*

And then he heard the *shtpp* of Basia's key in the lock. The chain was in place, but anyway the snib of the lock was depressed, so the apartment door couldn't be opened from the outside. *Shtpp.* There was a faint jingle of keys as Basia checked she was using the right one. *Shtpp. Shtpp.*

Piotr laid his finger against his lips – and smelled the rankness of Agnieszka's genitals. He leaned towards her, shaking his head vigorously when she tried to kiss him. 'No,' he whispered in her ear. 'She'll go away in a minute. Just wait quietly. Then you can leave.' They listened to the sibilance, not even daring to dress. A minute passed. Neither of them heard Basia's steps descending the concrete stairs. Piotr found himself listening for the terse resonance of the steel banister when it was slapped.

Shtpp. 'Shit', then, raising her voice, 'Piotr, are you in there?'

Basia began to thump on the door. After only a minute the hammering stopped and they heard the voice of the old woman in the apartment below. 'He's there with that woman he brings. It's disgusting. You should get a divorce.'

'You should mind your own fucking business,' Basia yelled. 'Piotr, open the bloody door, you shit.'

They began to get dressed. Agnieszka's raincoat was still dark over the shoulders from the rain. She tightened the belt and looked at Piotr. He was folding away the sofa bed.

'Deny it,' he whispered. 'Say we weren't doing anything, but it looked bad, so we kept quiet. In case she came to the wrong conclusion.'

Agnieszka shook her head. 'No. It's fate, Piotr. Tell her you love me. That you're leaving her.' But she was pale.

'I can't.'

Agnieszka wound up her lipstick, applied its apricot shimmer with a surprisingly steady hand, turned up the collar of her raincoat and went to open the door. 'I am not going to discuss our love with her. My conscience is clear. And yours should be, too. I'm going home. How could something so beautiful between us, something so noble, be touched by something so grubby? So undignified?'

The door opened, but there was no sign of Basia, only the head of the old woman, at floor level, staring up through the bars like a criminal.

Agnieszka stepped out and received an almighty crack to the side of her head from the handle of Basia's red umbrella. The old woman applauded. Agnieszka did not collapse. She held on to the ochre banister with both hands, leaning forward, as if she were keeping it at arm's length. Her mouth opened and shut, opened and shut. Tears brimmed in her eyes.

Piotr was amazed to find himself noticing the sleeve belts on her raincoat – how they gathered the cuffs – *like Christmas crackers.*

31

Without saying a word, or even acknowledging Basia's existence, Agnieszka walked slowly down the stairs.

———————

At about the same time that Piotr, watched by the old woman from the floor below, was turning to face his wife, Basia, Ryszard (Rysiek) Harlan had almost completed the restoration of the family palace in Lublin.

Ten years ago, after decades of Communist neglect, everything – every wooden window frame, every outside door, including the double double-doors of the main entrance, and the elaborate ironwork of the gates – was scrofulous, leprous with broken paint. As if a sepia snapshot were fractionally out of focus. Ryszard remembered poetry readings in the palace – how he would oil the hinges like a fencer during the recitals to minimise the disruption of latecomers. His long oil can reaching like a rapier.

Rysiek was 54 when he fell in love with his 22-year-old dentist.

(So young a dentist? Yes: qualified after a two-year intensive training course run by the Polish air force for selected civilians as well as military personnel. A crash course.)

One June morning he watched her take a fresh pair of milk-coloured surgical gloves from the oblong cardboard dispenser, as anyone else might rustle out a tissue. He could see the washed-out ghost of her wristwatch, her young skin and fine eyebrows. There was a small bloom on her left-hand spectacle lens, which came and went as she breathed under her mask. Her neck was solid, without a wrinkle, and the creamy white of Horlicks except for a single small mole.

She held the hypodermic just out of his line of sight. As all dentists do. Like devious Cupids, pretending pain isn't on offer.

Of course, his mouth – its maculate teeth, plaque, receding gums, the blood-darned polyp inside his right-hand cheek – was scarcely an inspiration to love. No, she liked him because he laughed when she couldn't at first fix and afterwards remove the adjustable band around the canine to be filled. He watched the play of muscle in her arms as she worked it in and out of place.

'Your teeth are very close together,' she said, as she passed a length of dental floss between the teeth. 'Why did you laugh?'

'Just imagined spending the rest of my life with a mouth full of metal rods, wagging away while I talked.'

He could see she was smiling under the pleats of her paper mask.

———

Mouths.

Two weeks later, eagerly, anxiously almost, Rysiek was chewing a pellet of chewing gum – wormed out of the tight packet with finger and thumb – when a small piece broke off his left underside back molar. The mute babble of his lips slowed down. For a second or two, before he spat it out, the chewing gum was crunchy with bone, then gritty with eggshell. Rysiek explored with his tongue. Was it a filling? It was the tooth – whose rough plateau had acquired a plummet of ravine.

In the mirror over the basin in the Miciewicz Theatre men's toilets, however, he could barely see the damage – the graph of a stock market crash – so attentively traced, so lavishly reported, by his tongue. There was his tanned face, his carefully groomed greying beard, his alert, humorous, brown eyes, his ageing, tended teeth. He looked his age – 54 – because he was bald, but otherwise he looked vigorous and healthy. Deceptively so, he felt.

That same evening, in the palace, while he was simply talking to Véra, his wife, the filling in the troublesome tooth came out – leaving an Etna behind it. As Rysiek examined the amalgam chip of gravel – its burnished topside, its black magma underside – he saw through the mercury darkly the face of his new dentist.

Focus in her flecked, green eyes. The clear skin. The dense, charcoal eyelashes. Her one pointed elfin ear. He imagined a blade of grass wedged between her wet front teeth, conducting her conversation as her lips moved. And moved again. And moved. Each word a different configuration. The word made flesh. The word writ large.

Rysiek felt not like a lover but a man suddenly deaf, watching the mouth for its every meaning, its subtle, significant manoeuvres. Its endless Kama Sutra of sexual shapes.

'Shit, Véra. I'll phone in the morning and make an appointment.'

She opened a kitchen cupboard and reached up a can of olive oil. Slop of noise against the tin. Her sleeveless dress showed the swag of her upper arm.

Rysiek wasn't impotent – Véra's mouth was a maestro – but he wasn't nineteen any more.

They had no children. And they felt no great need for children. Certainly not enough to establish why Véra had never become pregnant during their long married life. They never consulted a doctor. Nor did they discuss it between themselves. In this marriage, their lack of discussion, their silence, was not one of avoidance, but of unsurprised agreement. They weren't afraid to quarrel. But they didn't quarrel. They got on well. Nor was Véra simply deferring to Rysiek because it was easier. It was easier, but she genuinely trusted him. They were content.

Her family was old Polish aristocracy that went back to the eighteenth century. With the post-war advent of Communism, the family palace in Lublin was divided, half into communal flats, half into a paint factory. Rysiek's family were workers – nice, simple people who ate at the table like derricks, weight on the left elbow, hunched, confidential. Their body odours were pungent and undisguised. Rysiek's mother had a nervous sniff. Rysiek, though, was strangely refined – an odourless, fastidious man, with a feeling for elegance, who sat straight up and held his knife like a surgeon, not like a clerk. Looking at Véra and Rysiek together, you might easily think that he, not she, was the aristocrat.

They had met thirty years ago at printing school in Łódz – and married. Equally without discussion, it seemed, looking back on those two smiling figures, holding hands, saying little. Rysiek clean-shaven then, Véra looking at the three hands in her lap. Their income came from specialised printing – limited editions with commissioned illustrations by reputable artists, etchings, woodcuts, dry points, which they sold abroad to collectors and rich libraries. They had their own printing press in a two-room flat on the seventeenth floor of a government housing block. The weight of machinery was a real risk to the occupants below. They made their own paper. The kitchen contained a tank in which the linen rags were pulped. It felt like a pond poisoned with algae – heavy, gelatinous, drowned in itself. Every week, in addition to the minimal rent, they paid off Pawel, the gat-toothed official in the housing department who had falsified the register.

———

Rysiek made an appointment to have his molar fixed, but bumped into his dentist the next day – literally, at lunchtime, while doing lengths at the swimming pool, she going in one direction, he the other. Both were doing the crawl. Their right arms clashed at the elbow, linked like a Scottish reel. In her pink goggles, nose clip and rubber-petalled bathing hat, Rysiek didn't recognise her.

'Sorry. Difficult to see when you're doing crawl.' He pinched his nose and blinked the chlorinated water out of his eyes.

'No, my fault, I …' She recognised him. 'Oh, *hi*. Pan Harlan. Jadwiga Kontrym.'

A different disguise – not the surgical yashmak. Rysiek opened his lips but said nothing.

'Your new dentist?' she reminded him interrogatively.

'Yes. I have an appointment. Tomorrow, actually.' He spoke quite slowly. As if he were recalling her personal details. Which he was, because now Jadwiga was so different – unattractive but mesmeric. The crow's-feet at her armpit. Her cold skin, blue pink, like a washed-out fruit stain. The upper curve of one breast – cold, coarse, granular – swelled from her navy costume. The hollow at the base of her throat held a little stoup of water. He had to stop himself dipping a finger in it.

She lifted the goggles on to her forehead. 'Really? I haven't looked. Alicia does all that. That's the receptionist.'

'Véra. That's my wife's name, too.'

'No. *Alicia*,' she laughed. 'Water in your ears.'

Her black eyelashes were wet calligraphy – asymmetrically peaked – like single, subtly different Arabic letters.

His lips moved a fraction, like a silent reader. As if deciding what to say. And then he took her wrist between his thumb and forefinger, firmly, to avoid a collision with another swimmer – pulling her towards him. 'Whoops.' They were nudged by the weight of the water, washing between them, touching them both.

As his fingers closed on her wrist, he noticed a nipple gather under the lycra.

Or was it already hard with the cold?

'Would you like coffee?'

'OK,' she smiled. 'But first I have to do five, no, *seven* more lengths.'

They discussed her sponsored swim for charity – Liver Cancer Awareness – and the next day, in the afternoon, she rebuilt his molar and warned him that when it happened again, he'd probably need a crown.

Rysiek agreed to sponsor a further hundred miles at ten zlotys a mile – a figure and a sum he was to increase in the months to come.

She was eighteen and very scared.

On the perfect porcelain of the toilet bowl there was a red solar system. Separate, circular planets. Single-speck stars. Bright, silent, beautiful, composed.

And the first sign of liver cancer.

Obviously, she needed to see a doctor, but Natalia was in Florence and it was a Sunday. Her *Rough Guide* lay on the bedside table – still damp from when it had slipped off the rocks into the sea at Marina di Pisa. She folded back a shutter to read it. Even at ten in the morning, the sun was so bright she had to squint at the book. It was difficult to turn the thick pages. She decided to go to the Emergency Department of the Ospedale near the English Cemetery because it was the nearest. Her travel insurance documents were in the waterproof compartment of her rucksack. She folded and wedged them into the zipped bit of her handbag where she kept her passport. There was no strength in her hands, she was sweating and her mouth was dry. She was conscious of her heart.

She showered. It was August. There was a water shortage. Turning to catch the trickle, she was like a model posing for photographs, obeying instructions – right shoulder up, head back to rinse her throat, left hand cupping her right breast, left shoulder up, face turned … She was eighteen and very beautiful. Leaving the tiny *pensione* off Santa Croce, her long wet tapering hair reached down her back like a bronze icicle. By the time she found the Ospedale, it was its usual buoyant blonde cloak.

The Ospedale seemed almost deserted and rather dark. She took off her sunglasses and pushed through the heavy black rubber doors with their dim plastic windows and followed the green arrows along the silent, faintly spongy corridors. At Reception, there was a nurse with a slight cast in her left eye. At first Natalia thought she was shaking the mercury down a thermometer. Closer to, she saw it was a phial of mascara. '*Sì?*'

Natalia explained in English that, after she had passed a motion this morning, she had noticed copious bleeding from the rectum. The nurse put a finger to her lips and pointed to an empty row of plastic chairs. Then she tapped the watch safety-pinned above her left nipple and held up four fingers.

In less than two minutes, she returned with a good-looking young doctor, small, tanned and slim in his green scrubs and espadrilles. His English wasn't much better than the nurse's. So Natalia explained in hesitant Italian that there was blood in her back exit when she took out the rubbish.

He shook his head and held his puzzled hands apart, smiling faintly. '*Non capisco.*'

Her grey-blue eyes filled. '*Gabinetti. Rosso.*'

The young doctor looked grave. '*Sì, capisco.* Come.'

The blinds of the examination room blinked shut. The doctor pulled out a lamp on its trellis extension from the wall. From a dispenser, he tore off two metres of rough green paper and spread it on the plastic couch. His right arm indicated the couch with an operatic gesture. 'Take off your clothez. Thank you. Lie down so. Thank you.' And he left, chivvying the curtains around her. Natalia took off her jeans and knickers and lay on her front as he had indicated.

It was nearly ten minutes before the doctor returned with six other doctors, who for twenty minutes inspected her in turn, conferred and re-examined her internally one after another. After further quietly intense discussion, she was told she could get dressed and go home because, in their opinion, there was nothing serious.

No, there was no charge. They waved away her medical insurance. The small polythene-lined bin beside the couch was almost half full with discarded surgical gloves, the colour of milk.

———

'You shouldn't swim so much. Your eyes are getting bloodshot,' Véra said. She was in the kitchen – the only modern room in the palace – making pear ice cream and raspberry ice cream from the fresh fruit.

'I need some goggles. It's the kids, pissing in the pool.' Rysiek's reply was lost in the noise of the blender, where consonants gave way to an all-purpose, high-pitched vowel. Jadwiga's eyes were the white of willow-pattern plates.

'You stink of chlorine, too.' As she passed, Véra stooped to kiss Rysiek's tanned bald head. Smooth as a ladies' leather glove.

'The new dentist swims there quite often,' Rysiek said. 'Pani Kontrym.'

'How's your tooth?' Véra swept a babel of pear peelings off the table into the bin.

'Fine, I think,' Rysiek said. He felt with his tongue, his mouth an ellipse. 'She seems nice. Do you want to ask her to supper?'

'Do *you* want to ask her to supper?'

'Why not.'

'Is she pretty?'

'Not in a nose-clip,' Rysiek replied.

'Tell her to wear it to supper, then.'

What was Véra thinking? What was Rysiek thinking?

'I was thinking of maybe driving to Prague. To see if I can't get a chandelier made up for the big reception room,' Rysiek said. But he wasn't thinking of driving to Prague. He was thinking of Jadwiga, across the kitchen table. And then? For the moment, that would do.

'Expensive.'

'Yes. But it's got to be right.'

Véra was thinking about Rysiek's casualness – wondering how studied it was, how genuine it was. She could sense something subtly different from his normal cool dealings with the world, the fastidious distance he habitually assumed. But she also thought this girl, this dentist, was not a threat. Rysiek was too perfectionist to permit disruption. She watched him take a black olive, eat it, run his fingers under the tap and dry them on the kitchen towel.

'Invite her when the English poets are reading,' she said.

'Good idea,' he said. Then he took another olive, ate it, ran his fingers under the tap and dried them on the kitchen towel.

In fact, Rysiek didn't know what he thought. Jadwiga's charisma was strange because it was ordinary. Rysiek visualised her clean, efficient crawl. He visualised the way she hooked the costume down over her trim buttocks with her thumbs. He didn't desire her. Desire is like an Equity Card.

You can't have an Equity Card until you've acted in something. You can't act in anything without an Equity Card. So Rysiek was filled with desire for desire. For an Equity Card. In other words, desire is opaque until it is enacted.

Until you've eaten an oyster, you don't know if you want to eat oysters. But Rysiek wasn't a virgin. He knew he liked oysters. He was heterosexual, therefore. But in middle age, the opposite sex ceases to be undifferentiated – and he preferred native oysters to Pacific oysters which are imported in a strong saline solution. The best oysters he had ever eaten were Estonian not-for-export oysters. So, did he want to fuck *this* woman, this dentist? He thought so, in theory, but how could he know in advance? The proof of the pudendum …

On the other hand, there was his *theoretical* desire. Which depended on his curiosity. And his curiosity depended on – very little. He was immune. He was obsessed. The bloom of breath on her spectacles. Minutiae.

The two dark olive stones lightened on the white bone-china saucer until they were the colour of pâté. An umlaut in eternity.

———

The proof of the pudendum …

In his 1999 autobiography, *Prince Charming*, Christopher Logue initially omitted any account of his sex life. It was added to the final draft after Matthew Evans, the chairman of Faber and Faber, read the 'finished' typescript and asked why there was no sex.

Did Matthew think Christopher was being reticent? The

English gentleman? The unbuttoned fly but the buttoned lip?

Or perhaps that Christopher was a prude? When he edited *Pseuds' Corner*, Christopher frequently selected items whose fault was not pretentiousness but sexual indiscretion, a relaxed attitude to privacy. Anything even remotely flagrant offended his *pudeur*. This censoriousness was not incompatible with his authorship (as Count Palmiro Vicarion) of *Lust*, a pornographic novel – apparently.

Or did Matthew think that there *hadn't been* any sex to speak of? If this last interpretation seems unlikely, let me tell you about a couple I thought I knew well, now long separated after a hygienic twenty-year marriage. They seemed happy enough. If anything, her slight hauteur seemed counter-intuitive and suggested a sexual hold over her husband. She contemplated her many bold rings and flexed her fist like someone trying on a knuckle-duster. The wife was continent, the husband was not: his excitement came from full frontal disclosure of their meagre sexual circumstances. He didn't take a lover. His infidelity took another form. He betrayed her body in a different way. His wife wouldn't allow him to put his tongue in her mouth when they kissed. And she avoided appearing in the nude – because she had a webbed toe, a fact the husband didn't discover until they had been married for ten years.

In its way, Christopher's silence on the subject was truthful. Till he was in his late twenties, early thirties, sex was the absence of sex.

True, but in another way his silence was not truthful. The whole truth? As he writes in his autobiography, though he fantasised incessantly about women's genitalia and masturbated fervently, he was nauseated by the actuality.

Until enacted, desire is opaque.

Christopher's cure was an uninhibited girl with rubbery flesh who encouraged sexual frankness. He discovered his desire. Real desire had replaced all that intense, etiologically sound but, as it proved, exiguous and unworkable theory. Was it the rubbery flesh? Was it the frankness?

Even *when* enacted, desire is opaque to the outside observer. And sometimes the participant ...

And I don't simply mean perversions – the erotic possibilities of gas masks. I mean the basics. What is objectively attractive about a penis? What is intrinsically attractive about a vagina? Perhaps the nauseated Christopher had a point? But we need another adjective here. 'Unexcited'. The unexcited and therefore nauseated Christopher?

Neutrality, indifference, can easily tip over into disgust. *Ulysses* records Bloom's undeceived, undeniable, corrective inventory as he flicks through a pornographic novel: 'Armpits' oniony sweat. Fishgluey slime ... Sulphur dung of lions!' Bloom, we are shown, doesn't invariably feel like this. But sometimes he does. Sometimes we all do – because it is the truth. One version of the truth. A truth.

There are two kinds of misogyny. The first is a generalised dislike of women. The second is a physical antipathy to women, a dislike of their biology. A gay character in Alan Hollinghurst's *The Swimming-Pool Library* says: 'There are chaps who don't care for them, you know ... Can't stand the sight of them, their titties and their big sit-upons, even the smell of them.' This second kind, not restricted to some chauvinist gay men, is what interests me here – being disliked, hated, for what is a biological given. It should be easy to dismiss as pathological and absurd. But it isn't. It is wounding. Why?

Black people must feel the absurdity of racism, the injustice of racism: who can alter the colour of his skin? And yet generations of African-Americans had their hair straightened (as Chip Gates wrote in the *New Yorker*) and had to learn to love their given physicality. 'Black is Beautiful' became a slogan, necessary because blacks had internalised the negative white racist verdict on their beauty. It isn't difficult to feel ugly if you are made insecure.

Is women's fear of physical misogyny partially an expression of their invidious position?

Perhaps women feel vulnerable to criticism because of their own sense of being oversold physically. The cosmetic image is an edited image – sweet-smelling, feminine, etc. – and it conflicts with their more realistic sense of themselves, the dispassionate, undisgusted way they experience their own bodies. They are, for example, hairier than the publicity pack's promises. No one's armpits are hairless. Depilation is a way of being economical with the truth.

Most women have first sight of their own genitals in a hand mirror. It is odd how this image differs from even the crudest pornography. The tiny mirror delivers something different – concentrated, essential, shorn of context. The things in themselves, vagina and anus – divorced from desire, from passion.

Divorced from desire. Think about genitals – their desirability, their undesirability – before a divorce and after a divorce.

Undesirability. Alone, in private, this spark of uncertainty, of insecurity, is virtually invisible. No one is embarrassed alone in the lavatory, for example. The air-freshener is for others. Smell – here a synecdoche for all bodily effluvia – becomes obtrusive, embarrassing only with the advent of other people, particularly the opposite sex. Selima Hill wrote an unforget-

45

table poem, 'Being a Wife', which remembers her first sexual experience, the sense of adventure and her severally pained awareness: 'the smell of fish / I dreaded I'd never get used to.' The poem concludes: 'Being a wife is like acting being a wife, / and the one that was her with him in the past is still me.'

There's something Sartrean and existentialist here. Remember Sartre's waiter in *Being and Nothingness*? No? OK, I'll remind you. In Part II of Chapter Two, 'Bad Faith', Sartre points out that no one is a waiter in a café as an inkwell is an inkwell, or a glass is a glass. The waiter has to act his part. 'It is necessary that we make ourselves what we are.' For Selima Hill, this means that, although you pretend the situation is normal, although it becomes normal, there is still a part of you standing to the side of the role you now inhabit. A part which dreads not only the smell of fish but also the possibility that you'll never get used to it. There is always an *element* of pretence – because there is always a choice about the way we feel about our bodies. (An inkwell or a glass has no choice.) Acceptance implies its opposite: refusal, revulsion, rejection. Even all-welcoming Walt Whitman has a Swift somewhere inside him. We think sex is natural. It is and it isn't. (Breast-feeding can be pretty complicated, too.)

The uncomplicated, purely sexual transaction, we think, takes place only between the prostitute and her customer. In other words, it is rare. Or comparatively rare, given the small percentage of prostitutes in the female population and the *relatively* small number of men who use prostitutes. I guess, too, that the word 'uncomplicated' is probably inaccurate: there are, however, no statistics for unsatisfactory, *complicated* visits to prostitutes. But simple, straightforward sex also has its place in marriage – where countless purely physical exchanges take place. The poet Oliver Reynolds has a fine poem called '*Asgwrn Cefn y Beic*' in his first book, *Skevington's*

Daughter. The Welsh title means 'The Crossbar of a Bike' and the poem describes a man fucking his girlfriend while she continues reading Flann O'Brien's *The Third Policeman.* In fact, it is a second fuck: 'A while now since he dismounted' is the first line. The crossbar. Leg-over. We've all been there.

But not at the beginning.

The beginning is different. A purely physical transaction is *possible* – but unlikely. This is why we fall in love. (Or get drunk.) So we can *ignore* the objective penis and the intrinsic cunt. They are our servants, ministering discreetly to our wants, unobtrusively serving our pleasure. Love, at first, involves ignoring the physical. We are autocrats. (Later, of course, there will be a revolution.)

It is like the newborn baby's face, where we focus on the features – and fail to see the surrounding physical realities. Spots. Fat. Sticky eye. Forceps bruising.

Later, we admit the ugliness of genitalia, and desire enters a third phase: the obscene. This is when we relish the ugliness and incorporate it into our desire.

But in the beginning, we ignore the obscene. It is off-stage, not to be seen, away from the scene. Which is what 'obscene' means. We are centre-stage – with our airbrushed genitals like drawings by Blake.

This is Esther Greenwood, in Sylvia Plath's *The Bell Jar*, on Buddy Willard's penis: 'The only thing I could think of was turkey neck and turkey gizzards and I felt very depressed.' Unillusioned, objective. The penis itself, unlovely, unloved. I think of Marcel in *À la recherche du temps perdu* when, after a concerned telephone call, mediated through the Danaids of the switchboard, he decides to visit his grandmother in Paris.

As he enters the room, he sees his beloved grandmother but doesn't recognise her for a moment. He sees only a grotesque old woman with coarse red features. Then, tardily, his habitual love transfigures the ugly objective fact.

We need love. Love is psychotropic. It rescues us from ribald reality by telling us a rival truth. It is a beautiful beneficent necessary lie. Without which we would live imprisoned in our laughable sexual ugliness – in the cell of our cells. With it, we succumb and soar to the music of mucus, the song of saliva.

This is Gavin Ewart's 'Circe': 'It certainly is the smell of her cunt / makes you fall on your knees and grunt.' But that is later, not at the beginning. At the beginning, there is love. Without helpfully myopic Cupid, he would experience the burden, instead, of brilliant, fatal factuality – followed by shame and self-censorship. Welcome to the war of attrition, where candour confidently confronts its enemy: unsleeping, inexhaustible *pudeur*; where victory is always to the weak, the cowardly, the craven.

All sexual organs – male and female – are an acquired taste. Like Stilton. Like black coffee. Like oysters. Especially the taste of them: this is Selima Hill on semen: 'the peculiar, leering, antediluvian taste / I preferred not to taste.' At least, I think it is semen. It could be herself. The context is ambiguous.

Rysiek is before the beginning – afraid of the purely physical transaction, afraid of his uncertain desire, unsure there is love in his dentist's heart.

———

The two English poets had quarrelled before the reading and were not speaking to each other. They were having a glass of beer in their hotel bar when the younger asked the elder why he wrote so much about his adulteries. 'Doesn't it piss Heather off?'

'What *adulteries*? I am not a fucking confessional poet. OK?' He spoke over the rim of his halted glass. He set the glass down on the counter.

'Does that mean those poems about adultery aren't really about adultery?' The younger poet closed one eye against the smoke from his cigarette. He had been needling the older poet since they left Heathrow three days before.

'*Amour* fucking *courtois*. The courtly love tradition, you literalist.' The elder poet made deliberate eye contact, held it, then threw a handful of peanuts into his mouth.

'*Right*. Part of *that* literary tradition. Arthur crap in bed, so Guinevere goes off with Lancelot. The aptly named and indefatigable. Goes all night. So that poem about the woman who finds a pregnant vixen dead in a trap isn't about an abortion, then? "She too felt trapped. | She bled ..." Somebody told me that was really about Linda Twarp.'

Linda Twarp was a Canadian poet, living in London, single, now in her early fifties, sexually active.

'Who told you that? *Somebody told me that was really about ...* Somebody who?'

'Linda.' The younger poet blew a smoke ring. 'When *I* was fucking her. You're not the only one who's been there, you know.'

He was lying. He blew another billowing smoke ring. A *frisson*, it shimmied and writhed before it dispersed.

For Rysiek, this quarrel was not without consequence.

The poems were, of course, adulterous. But there was an accepted code of behaviour about apparently transgressive poems – which the young poet had transgressed. You ignored the occasion and admired the art. You weren't supposed to ask to see the Polaroids. The elder poet was silenced by the younger poet's apparently definitive answer. The desire to deliver a crushing retort was stifled. Aborted, you might say. There was an insistent, costive craving inside him. He needed to crush something, to pain something. But he wasn't aware of this imperative, only of a vague discomfort that would eventually make him want to discomfit – anyone. And 'anyone' turned out to be Rysiek.

The two poets read to an invited audience of thirty in the large reception room, the one still lacking its authentic chandelier. Afterwards, for an hour, wine circulated generally – before supper in the kitchen, for eight guests, including Jadwiga and the two poets.

Maurice, the older poet, could see his host talking to a young girl with modest, grave good looks. He watched Rysiek's full brown lips move deliberately in his carefully trimmed beard, as if his mouth knew how handsome it was. Rysiek spoke like someone being lip-read. Maurice wondered if the girl were deaf. She seemed to look at Rysiek's lips rather than his eyes. He worked his way across the room.

'It's very kind of you to have us in your beautiful house.'

'A great pleasure.' Rysiek didn't look as though it was a particular pleasure. Only his mouth smiled – briefly. 'The palace needs the sense of occasion. I was just telling Jadwiga ...'

Maurice held out his hand to Jadwiga. '*Jadwiga*. Poets are allowed to say these things. You are so beautiful, I had to come and tell you. You have the simple beauty of the first grass. Hasn't she?' He appealed to Rysiek.

'Jadwiga doesn't speak English very well.'

'Won't you translate my compliment?'

Rysiek laughed to temper his rebuke. 'Poets may be allowed to say such things to complete strangers but other people have no such licence.'

'But you're obviously *not* strangers,' Maurice countered. 'I've been watching you across the room. I was wondering what your relationship was. Certainly not strangers. Definitely something more intimate. But there I go, being the poet again.'

'Jadwiga is my dentist.'

'*Scandalously* intimate, then. Please, will you be my dentist?' Maurice asked. 'Before, when I was watching you across the room, I was wondering if you were deaf. Because he was doing all the talking.'

'If I are deaf, surely *I* talk – so I do not have to listen. No, I was not deaf.' Jadwiga suddenly grinned, unable to conceal her pleasure and her amusement. 'My English is bad. A little I understand. Beautiful like grass? Thank you.' As she repeated the compliment, red blotches appeared on her chest and at her throat.

Maurice was touched by her modesty, by the ugliness of her blush. Rysiek was jealous of the swift intimacy this ugly, red-faced poet had established – jealous of his manner, his offensive ease.

Jadwiga addressed him in Polish. 'You know, I think I shouldn't stay to supper. My English is not good enough, so this poet will just go on paying embarrassing compliments all night. It is nice for me but boring for everyone else. Maybe boring for me in the end.'

Jadwiga let Rysiek drive her to her one-room apartment on the outskirts of Lublin – a forty-minute return journey.

The party ended and the inner circle of invited guests went through to the kitchen. Where they waited and made conversation. About home-made pea soup and the roadside sale of mushrooms. Home-made ice cream would be exported were it not for contravention of EC regulations that made the use of fresh fruit illegal. The framed Dufy posters were admired. Dufy's calligraphic style was discussed. How his use of arbitrary block background colour derived from the lino-cut. The ongoing restoration of the palace, its courtyard structure, the absence of state subsidy were discussed. English food, Polish sausage, the British Council's role in post-Communist Poland.

At the outskirts, Rysiek was switching off the engine. He and Jadwiga had discussed the elder poet's writing – in particular, a woman stepping out of the shower 'like a rhinestone cowboy', a simile Rysiek said he didn't understand but which Jadwiga admired. 'It's the drops of water on her skin,' she said, laughing a little at his seriousness, his sulkiness.

'You didn't like him?'

Rysiek inclined his head. 'And now I've got to have supper with him.'

They shook hands before she got out of the car. He watched her enter the sprung glass door, which shivered shut. He rested his arms and his head on the steering wheel, as if he had been driving through the night. There was a tap on his window. Jadwiga. He wound it down. She leaned in her face and kissed him on the lips. A quick, dry, scratchy kiss.

'Thank you for the lift.'

And she was gone again.

Rysiek drove slowly, considering her breath. Its coldness. Under the residual sourness of the wine, there was something … faintly faecal. He eased the claustrophobic erection crippled in his underpants.

That old joke about dentists always having halitosis. And then he stopped smiling. Perhaps it was his breath, not hers, that smelled of shit. His erection went.

His erection *went*.

The difference between 'come' and 'go'.

He *came*.

A famous limerick: 'There was a young fellow from Ghent, / Whose cock was dramatically bent. / A curve so extreme / Was not in God's scheme / And instead of coming he went.' A famous limerick – of which I've had to invent lines three and four, because indecency avoids the public record.

In French, the word for joy, *jouissance*, is also the word for coming, for *plaisir sexuel*. *Jouissance* seems, well, less pedestrian than 'coming'. But the achievement of orgasm – or

53

orgasme – is <u>*parvenir*</u> *à la jouissance*. And *parvenir* means to arrive at a predetermined point. In English that is why we use the French word *parvenue* to suggest someone who is socially ambitious, someone who has only recently achieved social prominence, social *heights* – a social *climber*.

What has the social corkscrew to do with orgasm, *Höhepunkt* in German?

This. The connotation of 'parvenue' has widened to mean 'social climber' – but initially it meant not simply its process of upward struggle but someone who had achieved its peak very, very recently. A 'parvenue' is someone who isn't someone, but someone who is a nobody. Our other word for such a person is an 'arriviste' – someone who has just arrived at the desired destination. 'One of the low on whom assurance sits / As a silk hat on a Bradford millionaire'.

The idea of a destination is crucial to the idea of sex – once you have experienced orgasm. Before you have experienced orgasm, the cock is pleasurably lost. It isn't arriving, consciously *coming* to a desired destination. It is going, but going nowhere in particular, it is running on the spot.

Consider the difference between these two sentences: 'I went to Paris in 1953'; 'I came to Paris in 1953'. The first sentence is open-ended in its implication. The 'I' was certainly in Paris in 1953 but did not necessarily *stay* there. The second sentence implies that the 'I' stayed in Paris.

If we were to add the phrase 'on holiday' to both sentences, the implication of 'to go' is still not the same as that of 'to come'. Although the addition 'on holiday' suggests impermanence, the sentence with the verb 'to come' carries a charge of permanence – of finality.

Thus. 'I went to Paris on holiday in 1953.' 'I came to Paris on holiday in 1953.' It seems to me that the second of these sentences implies that the speaker is still in Paris.

But could one add to both sentences equally the phrase 'but only stayed for a day'? No, not 'equally'. For me, the second sentence, 'I came to Paris on holiday in 1953 but only stayed for a day', implies that the speaker is resident in Paris now. Or that the shortness of the 1953 stay has now been rectified, extended.

'To Carthage then I came.' T. S. Eliot's *The Waste Land* again, quoting the *Confessions* of Saint Augustine. Three neat iambs – created by the addition of 'then' to the Latin original.

Why doesn't Saint Augustine write: 'Then I went to Carthage'? In fact, the Penguin translation of this passage is: 'I went to Carthage.' The Latin original says: '*Veni Karthaginem, et circumspectrepebat me undique sartago flagitiosorum amorum.*' That is, in the Loeb translation: 'To Carthage I came, where a whole frying pan full of abominable loves crackled about me, and on every side.' *Veni*. I came. For an extended period, therefore. In Augustine's case from AD 371 to AD 383, when he left for Rome.

This idea of permanence, of coming, of *arrival*, is obvious in Wagner's great love duet in Act II of *Tristan und Isolde* – where music and singers strain towards a climax, and again thrust towards an orgasm. Which will be a *permanent* destination because the two lovers have a *Liebestod* in mind. You can't get more permanent than death.

In French, the orgasm is sometimes known as *le petit mort*. On the face of it, this seems at once morbid and inappropriate – unless you have sat by a bedside listening to a dying person labour towards their death and witnessed the physical effort involved in leaving behind the physical.

However, in Act II of *Tristan und Isolde*, the musical orgasmic simulacrum is interrupted by Kurwenal. In fact, the melody doesn't reach its full climax until Isolde's *Liebestod* in Act III, scene 3.

When Rysiek returned exactly fifty-five minutes after he had left, his guests had run out of conversation. Earlier, the younger poet had wondered into the silence why the word 'banal' was pronounced to rhyme with 'canal' – rather than 'anal'.

Before, he was 'relaxed'. A little risqué, but playful, not embarrassing. Now, he was drunkenly explaining why fellatio is called a blow-job.

'Just like *scumbag*. Which no one realises. Generalised insult, they think. No. A condom. In actual fact.'

The wine swayed in his glass.

'Same thing with a blow-job. You see, most people *suck*. Far as I know, no one blows. *No one.* Spite of the *verb*. Can I *blow* you? Really means can I *suck* you. Suck you *off*. And wank you off. But not *blow* you off. Because the blow-job refers to the gooey affinity between snot and semen, snot and come. Intertexturality.'

Because he was drunk, his muffed pronunciation obliterated the distinction, the play, between 'intertextuality' and 'inter-texturality'. Twice he tried to get his thickened tongue around the word and then gave up.

Herdwick, the representative from the British Council, smiled tightly. He knew poets were supposed to be 'unreli-able', but he was already composing his negative report.

The younger poet rubbed his nose with the back of his hand. 'Rather imprecise, I agree. But probably, probably a coinage from the gay community. Which isn't noted for accuracy in these matters. I mean women don't smell of fish. Except very very very approximately. They smell of cunt. In my experience. But gays call all women "fish", some gays. The misogynists. Anyway, some guy strokes his nose at you, happened to me in Venice, he probably wants to give you a blow-job.'

He grinned, loosened his tie and asked for an ashtray. Rysiek slid one across the table.

It was partly – but only partly, as I've explained – to cover the embarrassment created by this conversational essay that the elder poet asked his question.

Very clearly Maurice asked Rysiek where he had been for the last hour while his guests had been waiting. It was the question an exasperated wife might have asked. But there was no exasperation in the elder poet's voice – just amiable curiosity. As if Rysiek had been caught up in a political demonstration, or his car had broken down, or his mother had been taken ill. The tone of the question gave away nothing. Everyone knew that Rysiek had given his dentist a lift home. Véra had told them. So the phrasing of the question was important if it were not to sound rude.

'We've all been wondering what you've been doing all this time with your delicious dentist.' He laughed richly so that everyone would know it was a harmless joke.

Rysiek's brows gathered. 'I was driving her home.'

'We know that. But was everything OK? Did something happen?

'Happen?' Rysiek's voice was tight, unamused.

'I don't know, something that delayed you.' He grinned broadly to show he was teasing. 'Roadworks? A puncture, maybe?'

Rysiek shook his head very slightly. 'No. Nothing like that. That's how long it takes.'

'Very polite. Assiduous, even. The extra mile. The extra *kilometre*. You know how to be attentive to your guests. Well, the beautiful ones.'

The elder poet's expression was flirtatious, roguish, but Véra was quick to head off the hint of reproach. 'No one treats a dentist lightly in Poland. You never know when you might need root-canal work. Some guests are more equal than others.'

'I hope she was suitably grateful.' Again the rich friendly laugh.

'We won't know until we see her next bill,' Véra said, in a way that closed the topic down. 'Shall we eat?'

The younger poet pointed across the table to the elder poet. '*Amour courtois*, courtly love. You should know all about that. You're the bloody expert, mate.'

———

As Véra removed her eye make-up with a cotton bud, she addressed her careful reflection in triplicate. 'They were a nightmare.'

Rysiek was reading in bed. He looked over his depressed clericals. He dragged his attention away from the memory of that scratchy kiss. 'Can't decide which of them was worse.'

'The younger one was drunk. But the older one was poisonous, didn't you think? Trying to get you into bed with Jadwiga.
Trying to *talk* you into bed with Jadwiga. She's very nice, by
the way.' What else could she say?

Rysiek addressed the back of her head. 'She is, isn't she?'

He was thinking: good thing we aren't facing each other. Véra
was thinking: this isn't quite a candid conversation. It is full of
address. This is a careful conversation, an exchange, pretending to be casual. Why? She pulled down her lower lip the
better to view her gums. As she looked in the mirror, the adja-
cent mirrors looked at each other, and she thought to herself:
'This is a mirror image of the poet's conversation: apparently
playful but actually tendentious, and ironically friendly.'

Her lip between her fingers lent her the disgusted look of
someone poisoned in a play.

As she lifted the duvet, she decided to check. Would he flinch
away if she tried to suck his cock? – afraid she might taste the
dentist's detritus. In the event, he let her suck him off. Not a
trace of a trace. As he groaned and jerked, she thought: *Now
take a rinse.*

––––––

Wanking *off* and sucking *off*. Because the penis is *on*. 'Wank
me' and 'wank me off' are two different statements. The second is more conclusive.

Similarly, the expression 'it's fucked', or *c'est foutu*, *isn't* a reference to the process of being fucked – as if that were
intrinsically demeaning. It is a reference to the completion of

the process. And the fact that you can no longer do it. It no longer works. It is limp. It is 'broken'. It is 'fucked'.

Another thought. Women never ask to be wanked off. They ask to be wanked. Which says a lot about the relative readiness of the woman's average orgasm compared to a man's.

I first saw Christopher Logue in 1964, when he was giving a poetry reading at St Anne's College JCR. I was late. As I tip-toed to a seat, Christopher was already launched into a poetic film script where Christ rode into Jerusalem with his three-foot-long penis erect between the ass's ears. At question time, I asked him if he really intended this film to be made.

Yes.

Wouldn't there, I asked, be a casting problem with the penis?

Papier-mâché, dear boy, *papier-mâché*.

George Jacobs, Frank Sinatra's valet: 'He'd stand there, dry-ing off. I had never seen a white guy with a *schlong* like that. I'd say, "What? What you do, put olive oil on it when you were a kid?"' And in the same TV documentary, Mel Shavelson, a film director, said that Ava Gardner said that 'Frank only weighs seventy-five pounds soaking wet but all of it's cock.'

The word *schlong* is reserved for magnitude. No one says, he had a little *schlong*.

The names for the penis. Johnson, for example. A real name. So a joke name. Like choosing Osmiroid or Sheaffer as a pen-name. V. S. Montblanc. But implying that the penis is also a person in its own right. With a single-minded mind of its own.

Large enough to secede from the body politic. I don't think anyone says, he had a tiny Johnson. All Johnsons are mega, are Johnson & Johnson. Eight-and-a-half-pounders, capable of surviving when separated from the host body.

Boswell is famous for his *Life of Johnson.* In 1922, a century after his death, Boswell's journals were discovered in Malahide Castle, north of Dublin, and at Fettercairn House, Aberdeen – respectively the homes of Lord Talbot de Malahide, a descendent, and Sir William Forbes, Boswell's literary executor. They were published and edited by Frederick A. Pottle. They recount in detail the details of Boswell's casual sexual encounters and transactions. They are Boswell's *Life of His Johnson.*

And in Michael Billington's biography *The Life and Work of Harold Pinter*, we read on p. 17 that Pinter's sexual adventurousness was the 'subject of envious ribaldry' by his schoolfriends: 'Morris Wernick used to say that all he had to do if he wanted to go to a fancy dress ball was to hang his *youga* (Yiddish for penis) over his shoulder and go as a petrol pump.'

And in the *Sunday Telegraph Magazine* (29 July 2001) – a reprint from *Vanity Fair*'s August issue – Judith Newman observed Matthew Freud in his skin-tight Agnès B. leather trousers: 'how to put this delicately? – [they] leave no doubt as to the truth of something an ex-girlfriend had told me about him: "He was my first proper boyfriend. It rather set a precedent, an expectation that has never quite been matched."'

I *and everyone else* on the Ponte Accademia in Venice have just watched a ginger Pit Bull ascend the wooden steps – wagging the biggest dog's penis I have ever seen, almost human in its dimensions. There was no one who didn't look, no one who wasn't interested.

In the early hours, a young man keeps exposing himself by lifting his kilt at a wedding reception. He has a big *schlong*. Who is most impressed by big penises? We are all *interested*, of course we are. But I think you will find that men with big penises are the ones most impressed by men with big penises.

———

To Piotr's gradual surprise, Agnieszka made no attempt to contact him after she was hit on the side of the head with the rosewood handle of Basia's umbrella.

What did he expect? Obviously, she couldn't phone him at home. He thought she would phone him at work. Even if there were no one else in the common room – marking papers or drying their shoes at the wall-heater – he would adopt his customary neutral tone. His responses would be inconsequential. To her question, 'Why can't you meet me on Friday night?' he would answer, 'No, I don't think it's arrived yet.' Or she would ask Piotr, 'Do you want to fuck me?' And he'd reply: 'Not all the work has been completed yet, but yes, as far as I know, that's the case.' He thought this strategy might help to contain her outrage.

But Agnieszka didn't phone. He could, of course, phone her. In some ways that was better because she shared an office at the Film Institute with only one other colleague, an older, divorced woman she'd taken into her confidence. The truth was Piotr was afraid of her anger at his timidity, the way he had stood to one side – silent in the curious silence after the blow. That curt, wordless, forceful *dak*.

Perhaps, he reasoned, she didn't wish to add to the pressure he was under? It was unlikely: Agnieszka had no way of knowing that Basia had summoned the entire family to a discussion of his infidelity. And, in any case, Agnieszka's consideration for others wasn't often evident. It wasn't selfishness but rather a principled egoism. She believed in the truth of her emotions. The important thing was not to live a lie. Other people, consideration for other people, putting their feelings first, inevitably meant putting your own feelings second. Hell is other people, Sartre said. But Agnieszka's conviction was unrelated to existentialist ideas of inauthenticity and *mauvaise foi*. In her case, she could imagine telling a lie in order to live in the truth.

The concept of 'poetic truth' appealed to her – the idea of something not literally true but nevertheless ideally true. The slow thistledown of stars, for example, their drift and cling, was something that struck her with renewed force whenever she removed her spectacles – and was looking over a lover's shoulder at the Milky Way. Her favourite poet was Marina Tsvetayeva.

In fact, a week passed before she telephoned – to tell Piotr that the blow delivered by the umbrella handle had produced first a lump, expected by Agnieszka and therefore unsurprising, and then a tumour. Which was aggressive, according to the doctor. She wanted to be quite certain before she telephoned. That's why she'd waited. Her voice was quite steady and her tone factual.

Piotr stared up at the Instytut ceiling with its elaborate nineteenth-century mouldings and the Greek islands of damp. He could see nothing for the pulsing blackness that shrouded his vision. He was finding it difficult to breathe. There was no saliva in his mouth.

'Piotr?'

When he tried to speak, he could manage only a whisper. 'Agnieszka.' Her name in his mouth sounded like the scratch of a fountain pen.

'I can't hear you.'

'I was saying your name.' He began to breathe at last but his voice was unsteady. 'Tell me what happened.'

'You *know* what happened.'

'At the doctor's.'

'He says I should expect secondaries. It will metastasise.'

'So is there going to be surgical intervention? Radium? Or chemo? What tests did he run?'

There was a long pause. 'No. It's hopeless, he says. A death sentence.'

'See another doctor. Agnieszka, you've got to see another doctor.'

'I want to die. There's nothing to live for now.'

Piotr was shocked to find himself more worried about his wife than about Agnieszka. Somewhere in his mind he already thought of it as a vindictive tumour. And he wanted to know if Agnieszka had been to the police, whether his wife might be facing some kind of criminal charge, and how exactly it would be framed. But he did not dare ask directly in case he put the idea in her head.

'I have to see you,' he said in a low voice, without thinking, as if there were someone else in the empty common room.

'Only if you spend the rest of my life with me.'

'The arrangements for that shipment will require detailed forward planning,' he said.

'Is there someone there?' she asked.

'That is the correct state of affairs. The arrangements for that shipment ...'

Agnieszka hung up with a clatter. And she didn't telephone again.

———

Basia was frying chicken livers and onions in the tiny kitchen when he told her about Agnieszka's tumour. She kept her back turned to him as he stood in the door-frame. These days she seldom glanced in his direction – much less looked him in the eyes. She took a pinch of salt with her right hand, rubbed a trickle into the pan and beat her hands clean like a pair of cymbals.

'I'd take it with a pinch of salt, that tumour of hers.'

'Basia, I have to see her.'

'See her.'

On the wet chopping board, a few bloody shreds, seasoned flour with a red sticky edge.

'She might go to the police,' he said.

'Or a lawyer, more likely. See her. Find out.'

'You don't believe her, do you?'

'Doesn't matter either way. Whether she's lying. Which she is. Or if it's the truth, in which case she'll die before the case is settled.'

'What if it's a criminal case? What if it isn't a civil action?'

'Lay the table.'

Basia was tempted to tell Piotr about her own lover.

Just to balance the hurt. But she ate without lifting her eyes from the plate.

———

A year ago, when Basia interviewed Witold for *Curtain* (the Krakow performance arts quarterly), she was fascinated by the way he crossed and uncrossed his legs. Like a professional gambler cutting a new deck of cards. So swift and practised. When he answered a difficult question, he ran the end of his cigarette around the ashtray while he thought. The caressing threat of a burning cigarette was one of Basia's oldest sexual fantasies – an undisclosed but reliably exciting resource.

His face was almost ugly but he had the dancer's narrow hips, scooped buttocks, veined arms and hands. A grey suede belt, two centimetres wide, emphasised his minute waist. The sleeves of his T-shirts were cut high or rolled to expose the shoulder muscle above the biceps and the glistening wires of armpit hair. He smoked *papirosy* because of their stylish length and ran his long fingers through his black hair.

After the third drink Basia asked him about Nijinkaya's chore-ography for *Les Noces*. He fixed her with his grey eyes in silence until she looked down at the point of his cigarette, and he said: 'Look at my lips. Not every man in ballet is homosexual. Did you know that?'

———

And yet he turned out to be homosexual and they turned out not to be lovers. They were like Bill Clinton and Monica Lewinsky. Full penetrative intercourse never took place. Fellatio, cunnilingus, mutual masturbation, penetration with suitably shaped deodorants, even a little whipping – yes. Straightforward fucking – no. Never. Had they been married, either of them could have applied successfully to the Vatican for an annulment on the grounds of non-consummation. As could President Clinton and Monica Lewinsky, had they been married. What the President meant was 'I did not have full penetrative sex with that woman.' After all, the thing Clinton wanted to say was impossible to say on national television – 'I never fucked her, OK?' Everyone would have understood *that*.

Witold's apartment was small but empty. The walls, windows and ceiling were covered with kitchen foil. The concrete floor was painted silver, too, though it looked a very pale grey compared to the reflective walls. The large double bed was covered completely by one red velvet theatre curtain with a freeway of gold swagging along the right-hand edge. Witold had acquired it from the Bergen Schillertheater in Rügen when the building was closed after an electrical fire. The curtain no longer smelled of smoke. Witold had drenched it many times in eau de cologne. In fact, if you looked closely, it was possible to see in the pile a relief map of scent stains. This half-curtain took up half of the one room. Otherwise it was empty. It was itself a theatre set, an almost deserted stage.

The bathroom, on the other hand, was a wardrobe, a walk-in closet – except that walking in was impossible. It was a squeeze-in closet, a library of clothes on coat hangers on three horizontal chromium rods. You had to crawl to the lavatory. The shower was unusable. Witold washed in the kitchen at the sink, using an abrasive flannel and great splashes of cologne.

The oven was a cupboard for shoes, socks and underwear. His diet was necessarily restricted. Witold ate bread and ring after ring of cold sausage, which now and then doubled as a dildo.

Why didn't Basia and Witold actually fuck?

Men's cocks have the same variety as women's breasts – the full range. And yet they differ from women's breasts. Not because they can be harder. I once felt the breasts of an adolescent girl which were hard. Cocks differ from breasts because no man has ever wished his cock smaller. The impulse is always towards enlargement. Always. If the penis is flaccid, its owner wishes it erect.

This is Flaubert to Louise Colet (15 July 1853): 'Life! Life! To have erections! That is everything, the only thing that counts!'

When it's erect, he wishes it larger.

Von Humboldt Fleischer in Saul Bellow's novel *Humboldt's Gift* is based on Delmore Schwarz, who is granted the boast of a large penis. He hammers on the bathroom door of 'a certain Ginnie', 'a Bennington girl', shouting, 'You don't know what you're missing. I'm a poet. I have a big cock.'

There is an interesting, unconscious pun which animates the Bennington girl's bathroom door episode. Why is Humboldt so elated, so manic? Because he has persuaded a grandee, Longstaff, to accede to one of his schemes: 'he had been delighted when Humboldt explained that he wanted the Belisha Foundation to endow a chair for him at Princeton.'

Von Humboldt Fleischer, then, is well endowed. Thanks to a piece of unconscious wordplay.

Humboldt also spreads lurid sexual gossip about T. S. Eliot. As did Delmore Schwarz, presumably. 'About Eliot he seemed to know strange facts no one else had ever heard.'

Once in the Café Royal, I discussed with Valerie Eliot the homosexual interpretation of *The Waste Land* by John Peter – which was published in F. W. Bateson's *Essays in Criticism* but withdrawn when Eliot protested and threatened legal action. I was puzzled that Eliot should have intervened. His attitude to interpretation in *The Use of Poetry and the Use of Criticism* is that 'the poem's existence is somewhere between the writer and the reader': its meaning is a transaction between authorial intention and reader's conception.

His widow explained that he had acted very reluctantly on the vehement advice of Helen Gardner and Janet Adam Smith. So an Oxford professor and the assistant literary editor of the *Listener* – not Eliot – decided that a non-negotiable propriety had been transgressed.

I told Valerie that the article was still on the open shelves of the Bodleian Library. As for the substance of Peter's article, Valerie dismissed it: 'Nothing wrong with Tom in that department.' (Addendum: in the *New Yorker* for 30 September 2002 Louis Menand reviewed Carole Seymour-Jones's biography of Vivienne Eliot. In the course of his piece, Menand remarks: 'Eliot was happy in his second marriage, which seems to have been a case of complete love of the married type. ("There was nothing wrong with Tom, if that's your implication," Valerie Eliot once told an interviewer who asked why Eliot's first marriage had been a failure.)')

In Mrs Eliot's house there are two large oil portraits of Eliot by Sir Gerald Kelly, one in the living room, the other in the kitchen. In the living room Eliot's overcoat is arranged over his crotch. In the kitchen, though, the seams, the folds, the *mass*, are revealingly on show. ('Nothing is unimportant about a great man,' Schoenberg said, adding that he would have liked to see Mahler tying his tie.)

But someone must have said something.

It must have been an interesting conversation when the precisely clerical Eliot delicately approached the point. As he *must* have done, you think, when you consider Gerald Kelly's third portrait of Eliot, which can be seen on the cover of Roy Davids Ltd's *Manuscripts and Letters, Portraits, Artefacts and Works of Art* (Catalogue VI, 1999). There the crotch area is masked by an open book (a few bold strokes, perfunctorily dashed off) and its shadow (thoroughly occluding).

But perhaps the public and private manner were very different. All the same, Valerie once showed me a love letter Eliot wrote her when they lived together. It was immensely touching and touching, too, that Eliot addressed in his letter the oddity of his writing what he could say directly to his beloved wife. He says he is a writer – and so he will write. And now his widow has the record of his love expressed as exactly as Eliot could record it. She need not trust to memory. And also Eliot obviously wanted posterity to know in the end how much he adored his wife.

He wrote a love letter to Valerie every Sunday and left it by her bedside.

In his last letter, which I haven't seen myself, Eliot wrote to Valerie that, as an Anglican, he believed in the after-life. But in case they didn't meet when they were both dead, he wanted her to know that his life with her made up the happiest years of his life. Valerie showed this letter to the Eliot scholar Christopher Ricks after a lunch at the Connaught where much wine had been drunk. He burst into tears.

Bellow's Mr Sammler, in *Mr Sammler's Planet*, when confronted by the black pick-pocket's huge aubergine-coloured ('tan-and-purple') penis, later lets drop that he used to think himself 'comely enough' in that region, though circumcised. I imagine he is speaking for Bellow. Whose sexual pride must have been undermined by James Atlas's biography – which publishes, on the one hand, a photograph of an oil painting by a former wife, where the well-hung, visibly circumcised author is cavorting nude in a sub-Matisse hedonistic dance. On the other hand, though, there is the testimony of several sexual partners that Bellow was unimaginative in the sack. Uninventive. Penetration and pure piston-action.

Poor Bellow. In its way, for Bellow, this very uninventiveness was actually a triumph. Or so I affectionately imagine. In *Herzog*, Herzog's sexual shortcoming is his short coming – the swiftness of his orgasm, the brevity of the balling before. Herzog's 'selfishness' – as a confidante of his ex-wife euphemistically refers to it – is premature ejaculation. In many respects, Herzog and Bellow are identical. Were they identical in the matter of premature ejaculation, then all that satirised, uninventive, unimaginative vigor (the American orthography is tauter, harder) represents a sexual conquest over the self. Unselfishness. That 'comely', sizeable, inevitably circumcised *schlong* put at the service of others.

Inevitably circumcised, we say of Jews. Except that many of them are uncircumcised. For example, my wife's brothers. Their parents, an English psychiatrist father, with dissenter

71

and Quaker ancestry, and a Russian Jewish mother, decided that their children would be safer uncircumcised. They had recent first-hand experience of Germany under the Nazis. The elder son, was born in 1936, the younger in 1938. Both brothers are unanimous that circumcision is a medical barbarity, and that this, not Nazi anti-Semitism, is the reason for their parents' decision. Is there perhaps a scintilla of sexual chauvinism in their attribution of motive?

In Ira Nadel's biography of Tom Stoppard, we learn that Stoppard and his elder brother, both Jews, are not both circumcised. I think we can deduce that the younger brother is the uncircumcised brother. An anti-fascist, anti-anti-Semitic measure.

Derrida, the 2002 documentary film directed by Kirby Dick and Amy Ziering Kofman, discloses that the Jewish Derrida chose not to have his son Pierre circumcised. The film does not tell us why.

Paul Steinberg recounts in *Speak You Also*, his memoir of being in Auschwitz, that everyone stared at him in the showers when he arrived, because he was uncircumcised.

Painter Working, Reflection, 1992–3, Lucian Freud's late self-portrait, nude but for boots, brush and palette, was much complimented for its candour – Rembrandt wrinkles, the penis *en plein vue* – but actually it is impossible to say from the impasto whether this Jew is circumcised or not. If anything, the pigment proposes a prepuce, though one presumes the contrary.

Joyce's Leopold Bloom – a free-thinking Jew – refers to his foreskin. It sticks to his underwear after he has surreptitiously masturbated.

'This wet is very unpleasant. Stuck. Well the foreskin is not back. Better detach.

Ow!'

Why didn't Basia and Witold fuck? Why did they only 'fuck'? Partly it was Basia's concession to fidelity. Until Witold had penetrated her and ejaculated, there was a corner, a cul-de-sac, which was forever and only Piotr's. Partly it was Witold's sexual disinclination, too. All vaginas contain a natural antiseptic which allows for the safe introduction of unsterile objects. Like unsterile penises. Nevertheless, penetrative sex often creates vaginal infections – thrush, yeast infections, cystitis. The antiseptic is also anti-spermicidal, though not to be relied on as a contraceptive method. In Basia's case, the acid content of this natural antiseptic was high enough to produce an extra redness in Witold's penis – *verging* on soreness, though never quite achieving it.

Or it may have been the alkaline content.

How did Witold know this was the case if he had never penetrated Basia? How *could* his penis verge on soreness, without ever quite achieving it?

To explain this, it is necessary to explain the concept of fidelity, as Basia perceived it. Fidelity wasn't something literal and pedantic. It was a fundamental mental posture, the *essential* truth.

She and Witold *had* fucked each other. But only twice. At the very beginning. So the existential truth was that Basia was faithful to Piotr and that Witold's penis had also verged on soreness.

In any case, the prohibition on vaginal intercourse encouraged excitement, obscenity and perversity in other areas. Basia was able to preserve her virtue, even as Witold pissed, with difficulty, into her mouth – a purely mechanical difficulty created by his erection. Psychologically, they both wanted the drilling drench, the water cannon. In practice, the few strained drops were the perfect sexual synecdoche.

And there was another reason for the vaginal prohibition. Basia did not believe in the purity of Witold's heterosexuality and she did not want to give Piotr AIDS. So, rather than swallow Witold's semen, she told him to come on her face. Which he naturally preferred as a well-known pornographic topos. In porno films, ejaculation always takes place outside the vagina – otherwise the punter can't *see* the orgasm. The face is an inappropriate and therefore preferred site because it is degrading to the woman. The (mutual) desire for degradation makes the face the appropriate telos.

Did I say that neither Basia nor Witold discussed these things? They simply happened in sexual silence, thoughtlessly. Neither discussed nor thought about, except subliminally.

———

The reason Basia never told Piotr about her lover was that, by then, they were no longer lovers. Witold had found someone else – a man. Also Basia was deeply persuaded by her own fundamental disposition towards fidelity. More, her righteous indignation with Piotr would be compromised if she indulged her instinct for revenge and sexual counter-strike. As it was, she could count on everyone's sympathy.

———

The family conference about Piotr's infidelity took place one Sunday afternoon in his brother Czesław's new apartment on the outskirts of Warsaw. It was also the architect's 51st birthday. The seal on the frosted bottle of Żubrówka was broken with a click – of plectrum on fingernail. Piotr thought of Agnieszka performing her poems, head bent over her guitar like a nursing mother. He listened, reproved, to the rustle, the *sigh* of the foil cap and the single tut-tut it took to pour a glass. Soon the white carved wooden tray would hold nine squat glasses – their clarity iced to ground glass – which would leave broken links of damp on the wood.

Fuck all this pathetic fucking pathetic fallacy, thought Piotr.

Czesław hadn't yet put up curtains. On the twentieth floor, they hardly seemed essential. Piotr looked down at the builders' rubble and the canopy of cow parsley flourishing between the blocks of new flats. He turned back to the room for the birthday toast.

The vodka made for frankness. Basia's parents sat in their coats. Her father looked down and turned his flat cap to the right like a steering wheel. They were both hurt and surprised by his behaviour. They would find it hard to forgive him.

'I find it hard to forgive myself,' Piotr said.

'You've behaved like a complete shit,' his mother-in-law said.

'You can't be harder on me than I am on myself.'

'Anyone can be sorry,' his mother-in-law said. 'But the damage is done now. Saying sorry won't mend anything. What's that supposed to mean? *Sorry.*'

'His eczema's back on his legs. That's what it means.' It was Basia, defending him against her parents. He looked up gratefully, but she wouldn't meet his eyes. She was stern yet in a strange way looked more vulnerable than usual. Younger. Touching.

Piotr realised that she wasn't wearing eye make-up.

He felt outmanoeuvred. Clean-shaven. Normal. Criminal. Why had he agreed to this ludicrous show trial?

'What we want to know, isn't it, is what he intends to do about it?' It was his mother-in-law again.

Piotr wondered why Basia's mother never mentioned the time – almost twenty years ago now, at a New Year party – she had kissed her future son-in-law and put her tongue in his mouth. He was standing with his arms folded outside the toilet when she came out, saw him, kissed him expertly and rejoined the party. Piotr hadn't been in the least surprised, actually. They were drunk but it wasn't a drunken kiss. It had seemed perfectly natural – proper, even – an acknowledgement of an ordinary fact. It was never repeated, never alluded to, written off by both as an alcoholic indiscretion. But the eidetic spark of mutual attraction was there for the first five years of his marriage and only gradually faded. They used to get on well, Piotr and his mother-in-law.

Edward, Piotr's younger, unmarried brother, said nothing. His sister, Nadia, also said nothing. She had parted from her husband over a similar affair and sat there like a reproach and a warning.

Piotr's father and Czesław spoke of the temptation, the *vanity*, of the male. Piotr knew they were defending him but their generic argument offended his sense of individuality. He wasn't flattered by the gift of Agnieszka's youth and beauty. It wasn't his vanity, it was his mortality that drove him. He

76

didn't want to remain young. He wanted to be alive before he died. That was all.

'The kid's told me how sorry he is,' Czesław concluded. 'And I think that's pretty obvious. He doesn't want to risk losing Basia and the kids. They're the most important thing in his life. He knows that.'

And Czesław put his arm around Piotr's shoulders. 'A toast. A toast to Piotr and Basia.'

———

But later, walking in the waste land between the new apartment blocks, Czesław was less friendly. 'You stupid cunt. What the fuck do you think you were doing, you prick.' The elder brother dressing down the younger. They faced each other. Czesław tore the cigarette out of Piotr's mouth. '*Smoking*. Why are you fucking smoking? You are so stupid. You don't fucking smoke.'

'You made my lip bleed.' Piotr touched his lower lip and looked at his finger.

'I don't give a fuck about your fucking lip.' Czesław threw the cigarette on the grass and ground it to pieces.

Both men were slightly breathless. As if they had been running up stairs. Piotr wondered why Czesław was *so* angry.

'For fuck's sake! Putting everything at risk. Your whole fucking life for a fucking fuck. I can't fucking believe it. In your own fucking house. Jesus.'

Piotr could smell cheese on Czesław's breath. He wanted to cry. He wasn't sure he could trust himself to speak.

'OK,' he said. 'I'll try to explain.' But his voice kept vanishing. 'The tests I had. Because of Ma.' He shook his head. His eyes looked up to the right. His mouth stretched.

'Take it easy, Piotr. Easy now.' There were tears in Czesław's voice, too.

'The point is. The point is. Shit. With her. I just think about her. Her cunt.' He was staring at Czesław's lavish tie knot. 'I want to live, you know. Before I die. And she understands that.' Piotr looked up and met his brother's grey eyes under the tangle of eyebrows. 'Agnieszka says we're like mayflies. We only live for an afternoon.'

Something changed in Czesław's eyes. A point of light.

'I don't know whether I should tell you this, our kid.' Czesław pushed his lips forward, ruefully. 'Anyway. But that's exactly what Agnieszka said to me when I was fucking her.'

The two brothers shook their heads and smiled at each other.

'Incredible.'

'It is. Fucking incredible.'

And they started comparing notes about Agnieszka in bed.

Three weeks later the affair began again. In spite of everything. And, in spite of everything, Piotr still believed that we are mayflies who only live for the afternoon.

Nothing more was heard about Agnieszka's tumour.

———

But cynicism and prudence had entered the love affair between Piotr and Agnieszka. How carefully he washed his cock with Lifeguard, a particularly pungent soap with a high coal-tar constituent. Now they fucked at the Film School on an improvised bed in a basement storeroom, next to a staff toilet. There were keys to both. Afterwards, Piotr stood on tiptoe at the toilet washbasin, resting his scrotum on the rim, as he eased his ragged soapy prepuce back and forth – wishing there were hot water with its greater cleansing power.

Cynicism lay between them like cold sperm on the single sheet. Like a map of the Hel peninsula. Piotr found himself wondering why Agnieszka hadn't suggested the storeroom as a venue before. Why in God's name had they ever risked the flat? Because, he thought, she *wanted* to be caught. So they could be together for the rest of their lives. So they could have children, grow old together. There was the mayfly's abbreviated intensity. Equally, there were the inextinguishable embers of a grand passion.

But Piotr no longer believed in their great exclusive passion.

Cynicism raised its unruly blond eyebrows.

It lay between them like his brother Czesław. Who had shared with Piotr a great many items in Agnieszka's sexual repertoire. Czesław who valued most – as did Piotr – Agnieszka's willingness to allow her lover – Piotr, Czesław, whoever – access to her fantasies. With all their shit and shame and trembling excitement.

Agnieszka was still a great fuck. A great fuck.

Piotr would send her postcards of the Picasso bathing hut series from the thirties and the illicit affair with Marie-Thérèse Walter. 'See our full range of swimwear.' 'Price reductions! Bargain basement!' 'Exclusive Key-Cutting Service.'

Basia, of course, knew that Piotr's affair with Agnieszka was still a going concern. It was the reek of coal tar. She never bought Lifeguard for the family.

Three nude self-portraits.

One of Stravinsky, two of Helmut Newton.

On p. 69 of *Igor and Véra Stravinsky: A Photograph Album 1921 to 1971*, edited by Robert Craft (Thames and Hudson, 1982), there are four nude studies of Stravinsky. Or, rather, three, since in one photograph Stravinsky is wearing a floral swimming costume and two-tone white and tan shoes. In this photograph, he is dressing to his right and his penis, though concealed, is three-quarters erect. Joe Orton, in the same spirit, stuffed toilet paper into his underpants for a photograph whose focal point was his enlarged crotch.

Picture 85 shows Stravinsky fully nude, left hand on his pelvis, apparently about to bathe in a river on whose opposite bank a white horse is cropping the long grass. (I say 'apparently' because Stravinsky never learned to swim.) Stravinsky's circumcised penis is clearly visible. The photograph was taken in July 1912 at Ustilug in Russia. According to Craft, Stravinsky 'seems to have sent copies of this photograph to Maurice Delage and Florent Schmitt'.

The more revealing caption, however, is appended to a more anodyne nude photograph of Stravinsky's rear. Viz: '1923 Château-Thierry. Stravinsky was proud of his muscle tone –

he did daily gymnastics – but perhaps this is not the full explanation for his having preserved photographs of himself in the buff.' Craft's implication, his innuendo – that Stravinsky was proud of his penis – doesn't really make sense here. Of four photographs only two display the penis. It is invisible in this photograph – where the only explanation, therefore, can be Stravinsky's pride in his 'muscle tone'. Had the caption appeared under the July 1912 photograph taken at Ustilug, it would have made perfect sense. Craft is torn, I should say, between prurience and privacy – both perfectly understandable feelings. He is both biographer and protector, exposing the truth and sheltering the beloved subject. So the innuendo is there in his caption but misleadingly applied to the 'wrong' photograph.

Craft previously addressed the subject in *Stravinsky in Pictures and Documents* by Vera Stravinsky and Robert Craft (Simon and Schuster, 1978): on p. 387 Craft quotes from his own diary for 8 August 1949 on the score of Stravinsky's earthiness. Stravinsky talks about farting as much as Mozart wrote about it in his letters. As a child he once ate his own shit to see what it tasted like – '*sans goût*'. Craft reports that this incident had been described by Stravinsky 'three times this summer'. 'It might also be concluded by anyone who happened to see Stravinsky's surprisingly large collection of photographs of himself in the nude that he is exhibitionistic. Certainly he likes sunbathing and is proud of his muscles, but, at the same time, he does not bother to cover himself, or to wear a bathing suit – which he does not have, in any case, since he cannot swim.' According to Craft, Stravinsky's conversation made frequent references to his penis (*poire*/syringe). The 'full explanation', we infer from all this, is Stravinsky's sexual exhibitionism in addition to his physical pride.

81

In Issue 25 of *Areté*, Robert Craft gave an interview in which he was asked if Stravinsky's penis was 'fluffed' for the nude photographs. He conceded it might be.

'It doesn't give me a hard on': in Russian, Stravinsky's favourite negative critical judgement.

I wonder when his sexual powers began to fail.

Why has no one written about this inevitability for all men? In 1998, the year of Stanley Tucci's comically anti-climactic *Big Night*, Brian Podmore was so depressed I went to Umbria especially to see him. Brian made his money, or some of it, by repositioning 'Personnel Management' as Human Resources. He invented the trade name Mandragorax. He was a design consultant, the son of the man who invented design consultancy, and described his work as 'selling hope – in a bottle'. Yes. For over fifteen years he'd been suffering from motor neurone disease – a very long time to survive the onset of that disease. He worked from home – a palatial converted farmhouse about thirty miles from Grosseto, at the end of a dark avenue of cypresses. Brian designed a sprinkler system to lay the dust. Cars set off the system as they approached his gates. 'I like my cypresses the black-brown of the perfect ristretto.' In his bathroom, there was a suit of transparent polyurethane armour on a chair, white or neutral rather than beige. Greaves. Breastplate. Backplate. Armlets. Like an art school schema, the ghost of a de Chirico.

Unarm, Eros; the long day's task is done.

He was in bed every time I visited and I noticed dandruff in his beard as I bent to kiss him. In a measured voice, he told me that he was depressed because he could no longer get an erection – 'Not that I would like this to be a matter of general discussion but I don't mind you knowing.' I assume that his complex medication made Viagra out of the question. The very last time I spoke to him on the telephone, I could hear his wife and the unmistakable note of tenderness in her voice when she spoke to Brian.

Her love didn't preclude taking a lover, whom Brian knew about, though not his name, or his profession, or anything personal. Brian managed to feel sorry for her lover and his minor role. It was the alternative to envy. Envy, not jealousy. Of his bit part.

Nor did impotence debar Brian from falling in love with a series of sun-tanned young women – women paid to read to him, who took dictation, who answered his emails, who brought the telephone to his ear – without in any way depleting the constant flow of love directed at his wife. And because he was impotent, he did not feel that he was lecherous – only pure, aesthetic, a connoisseur of beauty. Until, of course, he found himself wanting to see their fannies, wishing to watch them wank. He was like a man with an eating disorder avidly reading recipes. Sex starved. Hideously hungry. Tormented, deliciously, by all these *appetitlich* girls.

Gavin Ewart specialised in comic dirty poems. I've already quoted from one, 'Circe'. I remember a series, a comic bestiary based on words like 'the dildo' and 'the masturbon'. When we were in New York together, as part of a poetry jamboree in 1980, he told me he was impotent but sexually active, because young women, or a high percentage, appreciated indefatigable cunnilingus.

(I thought of Geoffrey Hill's strenuous poetic alter ego, Sebastian Arrurruz: 'my tongue in your cleft all night.' *All night.* All night in the wrong place. Or if not the wrong place, if better than nothing, if in the right general area, still not the ideal place. No wonder it took all night.)

Gavin's disclosure tells us something important about sex. We know the power of mind over matter in sex. We know also the power of matter over mind – how an erection affects our thinking, enables us to think the unthinkable, which in turn consolidates the erection. It is a symbiosis and a circularity, which is nevertheless not dependent on an unbroken circuit. Gavin Ewart tells us that, in the course of a lifetime, the mind is habituated to thinking about sex – addicted, permanently sexualised, easily equal to overriding a small disability like impotence. Why, otherwise, would impotent men turn to Viagra? Not simply to please their wives. Why don't impotent men lose the desire with the lost function? It isn't only nostalgia – the desire for desire. Desire itself survives.

This is David Hockney talking about late Picasso: 'Picasso died when he was, what, 91? Up until the last year of his life he was still painting in his studio. He wasn't very tall, probably under five feet, six inches, and there he'd stand, completely naked, in his studio, with his dogs. Imagine that puckered little bum! But what was he painting so ferociously? Huge canvases of female genitalia – the lot! Explicit, overt, sexual images. Now, just think what would have happened if he'd been in an old people's home. What would the nurses have said? "There's a filthy old man upstairs, bollock naked, painting disgusting pictures of women's fannies and things. He'll have to go!"'

Helmut Newton's *Portraits* (Quartet, 1987) has an introduction in the form of an interview between Newton and Carol Squiers, which took place in New York in the spring of 1987. It contains this exchange:

C S: 'When you photographed yourself in the nude in 1976, your clothes were very neatly folded on a chair in the picture. But when you photograph women who are nude, their clothes are scattered everywhere, in a kind of wild abandon.'

[*A non-question pretending to a vestigial feminism.*]

H N: 'I'm quite a tidy person. I would hate to live in disorder and I cannot work in disorder. But this is interesting – I create that disorder – I want the model to take all her clothes off and just dump them. [*Non-answer as both parties wonder if they can actually discuss the nude self-portrait: earlier in the interview Newton expresses his outrage when a woman photographer – probably Annie Leibovitz – wanted him to take his cock out of his pants.*] That self-portrait was included in a European catalogue, and I said to June [*his wife*]: "Maybe I shouldn't put that in – it shows how small my prick is. It's not very impressive!"'

Actually, there are two nude self-portraits in *Portraits.* One shows Newton's nude reflection in a hotel wardrobe mirror. The clothes are on the chair. A Hermès hold-all is on the bed. The photograph is taken so the head is cut off in the mirror. The cock is small. There is a second photograph (taken in 1973) of the nude Newton, this time reflected in a bathroom mirror, quite close up. His torso is covered with three electronic pads for an electrocardiogram at the Lenox Hill Hospital, New York. The circumcised penis is closer and larger – but not bigger. It is only more tumescent.

————

Rysiek was sulking. His hands were in his lap. He examined his palms. Jadwiga stretched out her leg to him and put her heel in his lap, forcing him to move his hands. He looked up

85

and past her. But he could sense she was grinning. He ignored the foot. It was beneath him. 'Go on,' Jadwiga crooned. 'Look at my foot.' Balanced in the space between the sole and the toes, there was a line of chocolate raisins. It was a peace offering. Rysiek took one and woke up. He dreamed about her all the time. Now he wanted to know what their quarrel had been about.

He brooded about it all day.

Recently, he had become very silent.

It was his silence that provoked Véra.

'I'm tired of listening to you and your conscience. Why don't you just fuck her and get it over with? Then it might go away. You know, it's boring – as well as painful – for me to have to hear you going on about her.' These days, Véra avoided her neck in the mirror. But now she caught its reflection elongated in a saucepan – muscular yet ravaged – like the underside of her tongue. Her mother's neck, an iguana's dewlap, lay in wait for her. Véra had reached the time of turtleneck sweaters. Of pashminas. Of silk shawls.

She found she couldn't look at Rysiek – that she disliked his youthful looks, his carefully cut beard, his trim mannerisms, his steepled hands, the way he put his tanned fingertips together, his air of calm. There was something of the cleric about him, something almost sanctimonious, which she eventually located in his mouth. It was the measured way the full lips lay together, chastely as an axiom. It was acting the abstract of a mouth. It held a pose of repose. And the ache of her suspense had lasted six months. She wanted to come to the destined place – so that the ache would go. She wanted what the massage parlour calls 'relief'.

To Véra, and to himself, Rysiek pretended it was conscience that was keeping him out of his dentist's bed. It was only conscience in part. It was mostly fear. He could list his physical imperfections as promptly as Véra his alleged advantages. The point of his tongue sought out the polyp in his mouth. There was a small firework of broken veins in his ankle. His skin was crowded, a tumult of blots, freckles, blemishes, red dots, tags, flat warts, moulds. He had one varicose vein on his calf. He wasn't young. This would be his first infidelity. Would he be impotent?

As a matter of fact, he would.

———

But how did Rysiek and Véra get to this point of frankness?

The last time we saw them, they were in bed, pretending. How did they move from concealment to revelation?

Aristotle's theory of causation is that there is no one cause. He proposes the hypothesis of a sculptor and his statue. The final cause is the sculptor's vision of the completed artefact. The efficient cause is the action of the chisel on the Carrara marble blasted from the mountain above Forte dei Marmi. The intermediate cause is the head of the hammer, the colour of twilight, on the sprayed head of the chisel. (As you know, Aristotle is very keen on metaphor. Just teasing.) Then there is the skill of the sculptor.

You see?

Rysiek is so used to asking her advice that the habit of a lifetime, of a marriage, exerted its pressure. It seemed natural.

Véra raises the issue because there is no sex between them?

And yet his handkerchief feels stiff and smells of semen before she puts it in the washing machine.

Or she is alerted by a suspicious increase in their sexual relations? Because he is trying to show her that nothing is happening elsewhere. Because he is trying to show himself that he still desires his wife. Because he is perpetually excited by the idea of the dentist and is using Véra as a valve against fornication.

She sees them together sitting outside a café. The dentist is crying.

Because Rysiek undresses for bed – the bed we last saw them in, pretending – and the dentist's thong falls out of his jeans. Inadvertently, he'd tucked the thong in with his shirt. It was so insubstantial he hadn't noticed.

All of these things – in roughly that order – changed the situation. Except for the thong. That happened later. Much later, after he'd told Véra the affair was over.

———

If we count the first scratchy kiss – through the wound-down window of Rysiek's Trabant – as a dry run, how did the first proper kiss come about?

Jadwiga had a boyfriend. Of long standing. Four years, in fact. He was a doctor at the Lublin Hospital, specialising in paediatrics – a specialism that left him with a strong desire not to have any children. He knew how vulnerable they are and, therefore, how vulnerable their parents become. Jadwiga wanted children eventually, ideally two, of each sex. There was something so settled in her assumption that the doctor wished to disturb it. She didn't press; indeed, she enunciated her conviction only twice perhaps. But there was something about her biological complacency that irked him. He felt there was an argument between them that he wanted to win. His reluctance to admit a vulnerability might have weighed with her. But his other arguments – standing there, polystyrene cup of coffee in hand, stethoscope awkwardly gathered and folded into the pocket of his white coat – weren't arguments so much as expressions of masculine reluctance to concede female imperatives.

'What is so brilliant about having a baby? Anyone can reproduce their idiot features. Idiots reproduce their idiot features. If we weren't so sentimental, we'd sterilise them. Why not write a novel? A play? Create something, instead of growing a baby. What happened to feminism? How can you let yourself be dictated to by your joke body? It is a fucking joke. Rudimentary genitals. Niggardly genitals. Don't believe that crap about the nerve endings in the clitoris as compared to the penis. Two food dispensers. And a womb – what is a womb? It's a people carrier. You're a form of public transport.'

He was a very good paediatrician – not only technically proficient, but his instinct around children, his *touch*, was perfect. He was patient. He was careful not to prompt them with possible symptoms. He could wait calmly, smiling, chatting about things they were interested in – transformers, dinosaurs, football teams, pop songs – until they trusted him. He listened carefully, sometimes hearing things they didn't say, between the words. And all the time, his intelligent hands were examining the patient, feeling their way, finding the pain.

He would have made a very good father.

He was a very good lover. It was those clever, patient fingers. The way he listened to her stifled moans so he might know what to do next.

And then he confessed to an infidelity – an infidelity he wanted to continue. With a nurse at the hospital – in the urology department.

'You want me to share you?' Jadwiga instinctively put up her hair with a pencil.

'Yes. I'm sorry. I don't want to lose you, but I don't think I can give her up. I've tried.'

He couldn't explain that, as his penis entered her vagina, there was a smell, a brief female intensity, a fine fugitive sexual essence he was addicted to. A dirty smell, close to carbide, which he wanted on his cock.

Jadwiga was telling Rysiek about the break-up with her boyfriend when Véra happened to be passing the café so she could see the fall of tears. They were too preoccupied to see her.

Pregnancy was Véra's first thought. Actually, Rysiek was explaining that it was possible to love two people at the same time. Though it might have seemed that way, he wasn't defending the doctor.

———

Sifting sentiment from sentimentality.

The American novelist Nicholson Baker lectured at Senate House on 12 March 2001. His subject was the need to preserve newsprint, which actually has a longer life than microfilm enthusiasts are prepared to admit. Microfilm has a shorter life than its advocates maintain, and it is inconvenient to use.

His initial defence of newsprint was to list and summarise some of the stories in the *New York Daily World* – including the saga of a man without a nose. This man had had various grafts from other parts of his body – but tore them off at the crucial stages and had to begin again.

Baker, having established the empirical worth of these newspapers, proceeded to name them – to name them as tenderly as a list of lost individuals. He suddenly observed a long silence. Then, a few minutes later, he was almost unable to say the words, 'These newspapers have just got to be saved.' It was very touching.

Nicholson Baker was touched. We were all touched. And yet these were only newspapers. They were not people. It was a sentimental moment.

Or was it a moment of true sentiment? I think so.

After all, it wasn't Nick Baker who compared the names of the newspapers to a list of lost individuals, as if we were at Yad Vashem. It was me. And it was me who then questioned its accuracy – as if Nick Baker were responsible for it.

Baker happens to care about old newspapers. They aren't in competition with people. Conceivably, he could care about both. In fact, the value of the newspapers resides in their record of human experience – that man without a nose.

———

But what about the first kiss? The first proper, properly improper kiss was at the end of a longer process than Rysiek imagined right at the beginning. The perfunctory graze of their dry lips together – sheer glass and brittle snag, like prawn shells – he had brooded into significance. On the basis of this polite peck, he fantasised a more elaborate future. And he was right: it wasn't entirely innocent on Jadwiga's part. But neither did it commit her to anything more concrete. It was an impulse.

But it was also a calculation. She had to return to the car to do it. The dryness of their lips, of both their lips, was a sign of something. That something wasn't relaxed. Or casual. Or matter-of-fact.

As soon as he discovered (by asking) that she had a boyfriend, Rysiek re-configured his expectations. 'Of course you have. It would be strange if you hadn't.' (As he asked, he had expected the answer 'no', because of the earlier kiss.) He became Jadwiga's confidant – Rysiek wasn't a man to compete – and that was how he came to be seen by Véra outside the café.

A confidant, but an undercover suitor, looking to advance his interests. He imagined placing his hand over her hands on a tablecloth – a gesture of agreement. Squeezing her arm, guiding her elbow, meeting her gaze, encircling her wrist to curb a heated denunciation and to give wise counsel. The difficulty was in effecting a transition from bedside manner to the bed itself. Rysiek found that silence helped, when listening slipped into silence. Silences stopped the thing from feeling too comfortable. There had to be an edge, an awkwardness, as well as this easy access. Access was better when it felt like security clearance.

In the event, it was she who kissed him. They were in the basement workshop under her surgery. She was showing him round. Labelled plaster casts of teeth in implausibly teetering, tittering columns. Stacked in the twilight, like a Sicilian ossuary. They were laughing but Rysiek had a sensation of emptiness, somewhere between hunger and anxiety, at the centre of his torso, his solar plexus. Where exactly was the solar plexus? She sat him down at the desk so he could see the X-rays of his own teeth. 'See how close together they are,' she murmured, leaning over his shoulder to see more clearly, so that her face was close to his. He was awake to the warmth from her cheek, the blood heat. But his mind had its own oneiric momentum. The exact location of the solar plexus? He could have asked her looking straight ahead, staring strictly at the slides. But he turned to her instead – and their faces nearly touched. She was so close he couldn't bring her features into focus. His question was forgotten as he felt her powerful gravitational pull. There seemed to be less than a centimetre between them. She parted her lips as if something was hurting her, but the pain became breath on his face as she fitted her lips to his and slid her tongue into his mouth.

He found he was gripping the lip of the desk with both hands. The moulding impressed itself into his palms and his fingers shook with the effort of trying to correct the tilt and warp of the world. This was what he had wanted for three months and he was afraid when he felt its force.

Jadwiga spoke first. 'I have to go to Warsaw for a week. To visit my grandmother. We think she's probably dying. But I wanted this to happen before I went.'

So Rysiek had to wait a week.

And then another week, because the grandmother died.

———

The surprise of sentiment. The force of feeling. In the grip of gravitas.

Rex was supposed to be at the Italian Cultural Institute at 6.45, where he was to give a short reading in support of PEN's work for freedom, with a dozen other writers: Tom Stoppard, Howard Jacobson, Beryl Bainbridge, Antonia Byatt, Victoria Glendinning, Phyllis James, Fergal Keane, Anthony Rudolph, Mavis Cheek.

Rex's extract was from Primo Levi's *If This Is a Man* – the passage explaining the difference between the judicially condemned, who are allowed privacy, peace and the time for contemplation, and the Jews in the transition camp, who were to be sent on transports to their grim destinations.

He'd drunk two gin and tonics at the Groucho Club between 5.30 and 6.30. By the time they went on for the first half, he had drunk three glasses of wine in the Green Room.

It struck him that everyone was reading too fast. Except for the final reader of the first part – Tom Stoppard, who read an extract from Albie Sachs's *Jail Diary*, itself a Primo Levi choice for his commonplace book. The extract turned on Sachs's release from jail – his initial disbelief, the gradual sense of certainty as he checks various possibilities with his former captors. Is he free? Yes. Can he telephone his mother? Yes.

The certainty of his freedom is established beyond doubt. Then he is re-arrested on the spot.

Stoppard read this slowly, with impeccable timing.

In the interval, Rex drank another three glasses of wine.

He was the penultimate reader. At the lectern he began by saying that Levi was a good man – 'and, I think, a great writer.' The self-important gravitas of that 'I think'. He delivered it weightily like a measured judgement. In fact, he had reservations about Levi as a writer, but the occasion exerted its own pressure towards the exalted.

Then Rex explained the context of the very short passage he was about to read. That Levi had scrupulously insisted he was not a true witness. That a survivor never could be. The only true witnesses had perished. They had entered the gas chambers.

(Isn't there something disingenuously modest in this scrupulous disclaimer? A phrase from Nicholson Baker's *U & I* comes pat: 'who will sort out the self-servingness of self-effacement?')

However, in this passage, short as it is, Levi comes as close as anyone would wish to heartbreak – terrible because it is also ordinary.

Rex began to read confidently with *extreme* slowness, as if the passage were a poem – partly because of Stoppard's example, partly because the chosen extract was so short that, read at normal speed, it would be over almost as soon as it began. And partly because he hadn't rehearsed or even re-read the passage and he was anxious not to make a mistake or stumble.

So it was that the passage surprised him – considered, the words delivered their world, its unfamiliarity restored. At two points – when, as a concession to the catastrophic circumstances, the children were excused homework that evening; when the mothers hung the children's clothes to dry on the barbed wire – at these two points, Rex was so moved his voice shook and the words had to be negotiated.

Moved, but also modestly, triumphantly aware that the audience would be moved by his visible emotion. It was Wilfred Owen's 'eternal reciprocity of tears'. And it was egotism.

As Rex left the lectern – feeling he had acquitted himself well, demonstrated his humanity – he suddenly wondered whether his listeners had only heard a sentimental reader who had clearly drunk too much.

———

Rex is at Orso's for dinner with friends. After a performance of *Ghosts*, Francesca Annis who plays Mrs Alving, joins the friends for pudding.

RALPH FIENNES: How did it go?

FRANCESCA: Very good. I moved myself.

RALPH: Across the stage?

FRANCESCA [*to Rex*]: It's usually *terrible* when the actor is moved.

Rex knows what she means. Her aside is a review of his reading.

Ibsen's *Ghosts* is about syphilis. By the end of the play Oswald Alving is dying of syphilis and imagining the convolutions of his softening brain as velvet. He has caught syphilis from Captain Alving's pipe, which, for a joke, the old roué makes him smoke – until he is sick. (In both senses: a hint.)

Syphilis shows a highly infectious sense of humour. Specialising in the slow burn.

———

'All invented proverbs are attributed to Iceland' – Icelandic proverb

———

When Rysiek and Jadwiga met at her large, one-room flat, it was all to do all over again. They didn't kiss. Somehow a kiss would have seemed artificial, a bit staged, not quite natural. But they talked about what they would do. They agreed to sleep together. She had been fitted with a reliable intrauterine device for her previous boyfriend, the doctor, the one who was paranoid about possible pregnancy.

'What kind of device exactly?' Rysiek felt it was polite to ask. He was preoccupied, thinking about the moment when he would have to take off his clothes.

'It's an IUD that releases something called progesterone at pre-timed intervals. It lasts two years and then you have to top it up. Actually, they replace the thing. You get a new implant. Don't worry, it works. My boyfriend chose it.'

That wasn't Rysiek's worry.

Rysiek's worry was his body – that inexhaustibly inventive comic genius.

———

In 2001 Ray Dolan was appointed to the Kinross Chair in Neuropsychiatry at University College, London. I attended his inaugural lecture at the Institute for Neurology in Queen Square, London WC1. The lecture was an account of an experiment designed to elucidate the body's response to danger. Dolan showed his subjects a filmed anthology of happy, reassuring moments. However, a single frame showed something frightening and hideous. Because it was only one frame, this image was physically impossible to see. All the same, the experimental subjects recorded higher adrenalin levels, increased heart rate – in fact, all the physical symptoms associated with extreme alarm.

You might want to explain this by citing Malcolm Gladwell's *Blink: The Power of Thinking Without Thinking* (2005). Gladwell argues that intuitive conclusions are often more accurate than considered decisions. He believes there is a form of rapid cognition, the kind of thinking that happens in the blink of an eye. The way we know immediately if someone is wearing a wig, for example. At Stansted Airport, queuing for security, I knew a man was wearing a wig, even though he ran his hand through his quiff. But his head never stopped moving – to stop you checking – which meant you didn't need to check. This is Leopold Bloom in Joyce's *Ulysses*, the 'Nausicaa' section: 'Sharp as needles they are. When I said to Molly the man at the corner of Cuffe street was goodlooking, thought she might like, twigged at once he had a false arm. Had too.' Perhaps Dolan's experimental subjects registered the single frame subliminally and the physical symptoms were the result of rapid cognition – those clever brains of ours.

Also included, however, in Professor Dolan's experiment were patients from the Institute of Neurology's hospital. These subjects were effectively without a brain – so severely brain-damaged they were incapable of any kind of ratiocination, let alone rapid cognition. These subjects had no brain to register the traumatic frame, even subliminally. Yet they, too, when shown the film, displayed identical symptoms of extreme alarm – increased heart rate, raised adrenalin levels and so on.

In other words, our bodies respond directly to external stimu-lae. The body knows things without the intervention of the mind. We know some things – even if only dangerous ones – before we know them.

The body has a mind of its own.

As Rysiek was about to discover.

In Ian McEwan's novel *Black Dogs* (1992) the hero, Jeremy, goes in darkness to a remote *bergerie* in rural France. In the total blackness of the kitchen, he searches for matches to light a candle. As he feels his way and rootles blindly in the kitchen drawer, he is visited by an overpowering sense of present evil. The candle finally lit, he reaches towards the fuse-box, as he has on many previous occasions, but something stops him. The knob is subtly different. He registers a slight asymmetry. Which proves to be a scorpion.

Ian McEwan and Ray Dolan are close friends. That is how I know Ray and came to be at his inaugural lecture. I am sure they talk to each other.

In June 2008 Sophie Hunter was in the Mexican jungle on a trek. She was sleeping in a tree house when she was stung on her little finger by a small scorpion under her pillow. The pain was acute, about ten times worse than a wasp sting. A numb-ness travelled rapidly up her arm as far as her shoulder. Then she felt as if an ice-pack had been applied to the top of her skull – a severe, dramatic coldness. This coldness continued downwards to her neck. Then to her heart and on to her legs and finally her feet. At this point, the poison began to attack her nervous system. She started – the exact word – to suffer involuntary muscle spasms, slight at first, but rapidly increasing in force until she was like someone having an epileptic episode with continuous violent seizures. She began to hallucinate. She was given an adrenalin shot when her throat swelled so much she couldn't breathe. Finally, an antidote was found and administered. She wasn't able to walk for four days and was carried out of the jungle on an improvised dooly.

Remote, and not remotely comic. But what about the black irony of dying to *avoid* being stung? Is that funny? Who is laughing, mirthlessly?

As we shall see, the fear of being stung can be fatal – and fatal for someone else into the bargain.

———

Rysiek undid the tinkling buckle of his belt and began to unbutton his shirt. Jadwiga undressed on the other side of the bed. He kept on his underpants. She kept on her bra and neat knickers. Neither took off their wristwatch. Leaving a puddle of clothes on the floor, they each got under the duvet from opposite sides of the bed.

They lay, silent, unsmiling, on their sides, heads on the pillows, facing each other.

Jadwiga touched the bookmark of hair on his chest with two fingers; then, with an air of decision, she undid the strap of her watch and laid it, a swimmer doing butterfly, on the bedside table between the clock and the little transistor. As she twisted away, Rysiek could see a dark brown raised mole between her shoulder blades, one white strap sinking in her flesh, and the strained, sturdy thickness where the bra fastened.

She turned back again and, looking at the ceiling, slightly arching her spine, deftly undid her bra, modestly, invisibly, without disturbing the duvet, then reached out an arm and deposited it on the floor beside the bed. Like an escapologist. Raising her knees and feet, she rolled down her pants and pushed them to the bottom of the bed. Rysiek could imagine them there, a white twist of cotton like a scrunchie.

'Now you,' she said, smiling.

He dipped his middle finger in the stoup at the base of her neck and danced a capering cross – forehead, diaphragm, shoulders.

'Ever since I saw you in the swimming pool I've wanted to do that,' he said.

'Now you can do whatever you want,' she said, deliberately, holding his gaze.

They kissed and brought their bodies close. He was struck – after Véra – by the smallness of her waist. Jadwiga was slightly built. As he reached down to hold one trim buttock, he discovered it was already slick with excitement. He felt between her buttocks, where it was wetter still. Rysiek had never known arousal on this scale. But, then, he hadn't known many women. Two, apart from Véra – before Véra. Extensive sexual experience, though, would only have told him such a thing was extraordinary.

His penis wasn't becoming erect. Far from getting bigger, it felt as though it was getting smaller. An anti-erection. Nothing extraordinary about that.

Rysiek thought he had the answer. 'Can we swap sides? If you lie on my left, I can use my right hand.' And, he thought, you can wank me, too.

She clambered over him so he could see the sweet swing of her tits. As he kissed her nipples, he could see two black hairs, delicate as an eyelash, growing at the top edge of one areola. Then he began to masturbate her. Expertly.

Jadwiga reciprocated – without success. There was nothing for expertise to exploit.

After fifteen minutes she said: 'Is it all right if I come? I'd like to come now.'

She gathered the labia between her index and her middle fingers under his gently circling, alternately penetrating, expert right hand. Her features were concentrated, straining, ugly with thinking their difficult thought. Her breathing quickened. Her right leg shook. Her face flinched away and she came, with a gasp, as if she could hold her breath no longer.

Then she came again.

And, with a strangled *yes*, for the third time.

The blotches on Jadwiga's neck and lower jaw faded almost as soon as she lay back on the sighing pillow, eyes closed. But Rysiek's entire body was blotchy, despite the absence of arousal on his part, and the rash remained for a couple of hours. It returned on subsequent occasions, in gradually diminished form.

Rysiek remained impotent. And he was impotent for six consecutive weeks. An epic of impotence.

But not with Véra. He was omnipotent with Véra.

We all know about the trauma of adultery, the pain inflicted on the betrayed partner. But we need to consider the trauma of the adulterer, or rather the trauma of the adulterer's body. The adulterer decides to commit adultery. Sometimes after a sustained period of reflection. His body or her body, though, is in arrears. It is still committed to its old partner and it is traumatised. For the body, adultery is like being a lobster plunged in boiling water. Or undergoing radical surgery – as it is separated from one person and transplanted to another person. Marriage's 'one flesh' is divided and joined to another body. Think of a severed finger and sewing it back on – all those nerve endings, all those veins, all those chemical pathways, that are damaged and 'repaired'. Now think of a body being severed from a body and attached to another body. No wonder nothing works. Adultery is in fact like convalescence, like recuperation after major interventionist surgery under a general anaesthetic – which significantly reduces your intelligence for at least a year. So your brain doesn't work properly either.

And Rysiek's rash?

When Vladimir Nabokov committed adultery with Irina Guadanini in Paris in January 1937, he was so racked with guilt that his disposition to psoriasis dramatically manifested itself. In August, Nabokov asked for the return of his love letters. On 7 September, the discarded mistress turned up in Cannes, recognised the Nabokovs' hotel by the trio of towels on the balcony and sat all day on the beach, her silent heartbreak only yards away from Vlodya, Véra and the little Dmitri on his tiny towel. In the evening she left, without a single word said on either side.

Irina died in Paris in 1976. She lived with her mother in Montparnasse, published one book of poems, *Pis'ma* (the Russian for 'letters'), and made a living as a poodle trimmer – giving dogs the look of a high-court judge in his full-bottomed wig. There is a theory that she went to Cannes because she was carrying Nabokov's child – someone known as Jacques Tenier, whose father on the birth certificate is identified only as BHC. In Cyrillic, BHC could stand for Vladimir Nabokov-Sirin.

The psoriasis, however, is a fact. His thickened, tumescent epidermis with the texture of a Twiglet.

Rysiek became adept at the improvised dildo – the parono-masiac deodorant, for example – the doppelgänger shampoo bottle. He was prepared to take the hint from the manufac-turer. And he was confident enough to resist Viagra. If only just confident enough. It was a near thing.

How do we get a hard-on? Adolescents often ask a different question: how do I get rid of this hard-on? Which makes it sound easy. As, of course, for adolescents it is – until the male encounters an actual member of the opposite sex. Then the possibilities for malfunction multiply dramatically. My own first act of intercourse lasted as long as an orgasm. Or slightly less, since I withdrew immediately the orgasm began. Which was on entry. The first throb perhaps took place in the vagina.

At any rate, it was quickly succeeded by a great deal of washing and splashing and scouring out with a sour flannel. (On the bus home, I thought: 'Now I can write a novel.') The other common catastrophe is the failure to become erect at all as one contemplates the intense, the dramatic ordinariness, of the female body – in conjunction with the *requirement* to have intercourse with it.

The physiology of the erection is an elegant act of deconstruction. It is a state of contradiction – the logical expression of which is curiously appropriate, namely P and not-P. Think of a balloon. Put too much air into it and, after enlarging beyond a certain point, it will explode. What stops the penis from either enlarging endlessly under the pressure of blood, or exploding? The first thing is the tough, fibrous epidermis – its outer skin.

The second thing is the chemistry of the erection. Stimulated by, say, the weight of a breast in the hand, the action of kissing, manual friction, the penis secretes a simple compound – nitric oxide, or NO. Despite the negative implied by the chemical formula, it is the nitric oxide which sets in train the chemical reaction that dilates the arteries, allowing the blood supply to the penis to increase. The interior of the penis is essentially a sponge, which expands just as sponges do. As the blood enters the penis, the spongy network constricts the outflow blood vessels, pressing them against the unyielding outer sheath. Thus less and less blood is able to flow out of the penis, while more blood accumulates within it. The result? A successful erection *and* a potential disaster. When Wemmick's aged parent in *Great Expectations* grills a sausage at the family hearth, Dickens writes (playing on the pun inherent in 'bangers and mash') that it resembled a firework. You get the picture. Penis as banger.

What saves the penis from the fragmented fate of the suicide bomber? First, its tough sheath, its supp-hose. But just as important is the presence of an enzyme in the penis that continuously acts against the effects of nitric oxide. Its contradiction is so powerful that the nitric oxide must be continuously replenished for the erection to be maintained. Think of the Forth Bridge – which famously weathers as quickly as it is repainted, so that the painting is continuous.

Viagra suppresses the enzyme that opposes the nitric oxide. This means that the erection persists after orgasm – for an hour or even longer. The state of permanent erection is known as priapism and its consequences are serious: the penis becomes internally scarred and permanently impotent. No Viagra user has so far been afflicted.

———

Rysiek became very funny about impotence. Not to Véra. Only to Jadwiga – who continued to come, to laugh at his jokes, to tolerate his terrible skin, to be equable about his impotence.

This was more dangerous for Véra than satisfactory sex.

———

Most of Rysiek's jokes involved the word 'bone'. As he twanged his penis, he addressed it: 'I've got a bone to pick with you.' He accused his penis of malingering, of being work-shy, of having no resolve, no backbone. Of narcolepsy: Rip Van Wrinkle.

'Do you know how the expression "Lucky Dog" evolved?'

Jadwiga was sitting on the bidet, with her back to him, splashing herself with both hands like a delving dog covering shit. She shook her head. 'No.'

'Because the dog is the only animal with a penile bone.'

———————

Rysiek was wrong. (So was Ted Hughes, who also believed this to be the case.) Dogs aren't the only animals with a penile bone. In fact, most mammals possess the *os penis* or *baculum* (Latin for 'stick' or 'staff'). For example, the racoon, gorillas, chimpanzees, the walrus, polar bears, rats, gerbils, jerboas, seals – cats as well as dogs. In Alaska penile bones are often extracted, polished and used as handles for knives. The racoon penile bone describes a particularly beautiful curve, a serpentine S shape very like Hogarth's line of beauty. The walrus penile bone is two feet long. The standard work is by William G. Eberhard: *Sexual Selection and Animal Genitalia* (Harvard University Press, 1985).

My colleague Richard Dawkins offers an explanation, in *The Selfish Gene*, of why man doesn't have a penile bone. He relates it to the generalised female preference for healthy, disease-resistant males as mates. Many examples of non-human male 'display' may look like beauty, braggadocio and vainglory, but they demonstrate something more fundamental: health. Diarrhoea, for example – always a bad sign – is difficult to disguise if you are a bird with a long glittering tail. The untarnished tail tells the female, therefore, that the male is healthy.

It seems likely that the human male once had a penile bone. Our closest evolutionary relative, the chimpanzee, has a penile bone, if a rather small one. (And a couple of monkey species have lost their penile bone, too.) Why have we lost such a useful sex aid? The Dawkins hypothesis – more pleasing than plausible, he warns – is that the ability to achieve and maintain a stiff erection *without a penile bone* is a very good indicator of general health. Erectile dysfunction is often related to poor health – diabetes, neurological disease, for example – as well as the usual psychological factors, like anxiety, stress, depression, loss of confidence, over-work. Marriage. All these things can affect the hydraulic mechanism, the stiff staff of life.

———

This is Dawkins foreseeing an objection to his hypothesis: 'There is a possible zone [*sic*] of contention here. How, it might be said, were the females who imposed the selection supposed to know whether the stiffness that they felt was bone or hydraulic pressure? After all, we began with the observation that a human erection can feel like bone. But I doubt if the females were really that easily fooled. They too were under selection, in their case not to lose bone but to gain judgment. And don't forget, the female is exposed to the very same penis when it is not erect, and the contrast is extremely striking. Bones cannot detumesce (though admittedly they can be retracted). Perhaps it is the impressive double life of the penis that guarantees the authenticity of the hydraulic advertisement.'

The contrast is extremely striking.

Often.

Invariably?

Most men would like to think so.

And then, one wet April afternoon, after a long delay of just over six weeks, Rysiek's erection arrived. Arbitrarily.

Because it's there.

A curve more curved at the base. The frenum pulled to a peak like the top of a stocking. A brown seam the length of the urethra, descending from the frenum to roughly bisect the knitting scrotum, and ending at the perineum. There was a tiny crystal ball at the tip which she worked all over the glans. Spit and polish. It was a steep slide her hand slid swiftly down, slowed by the curve at the bottom.

And he came. Like a wubbering springboard. His ejaculate jumped the length of her arm. Eight diminishing gouts. The first too high for her to lick. Right on the shoulder.

Jadwiga remembered walking through a meadow in the Tatras Mountains where every step sent out a spray of crickets as if you were wading into the Baltic.

'Samuel Beckett,' he said.

'What?'

'The sequel to *Godot*. *Godot* was foreplay. In the sequel, he comes.'

'I like your curve.'

'Well, everyone has one.'

'Not in my experience. You're the first. Everyone else has been more straightforward.'

'Nothing's straightforward about me,' Rysiek laughed. He was happier than he would have believed. He thought he had been completely, almost amiably, resigned. 'But there's that bronze satyr with the enormous wang in Athens, the one everybody sends you a postcard of. His cock is curved.'

He felt twenty again. He wondered whether he should shave off his beard. Then he remembered that now he was bald. He needed the beard.

And, just for second, he surprised a reflex longing in himself to phone Véra – so he could tell her how well things had just gone.

———

John Updike, in his 1999 collection of reviews and essays, *More Matter*, summarises the current state of scholarship on the size of Scott Fitzgerald's penis. You can find it on p. 541. There is Hemingway's report on Fitzgerald's self-doubt in *A Moveable Feast* – thanks to Zelda's supportive asides – and Hemingway's own foreshortened assessment, *de haut en bas*, in a French urinal. Then there is the experienced estimate of his last girlfriend, Sheila Graham, unremarkable either way, as well as someone who sighted Fitzgerald's ordinary cock as his dressing gown happened to gape for the gape of posterity.

On p. 655 Updike reviews *Lana: The Lady, The Legend, The Truth*, Lana Turner's autobiography: 'If you want to know how disappointing it was to go to bed with Artie Shaw, this is your book.' But on p. 235 of his autobiography, *Prince Charming*, Christopher Logue describes being driven by Artie Shaw from an airport in Spain to the house of their mutual hosts. Artie Shaw stops the car and takes out his penis to show Christopher 'the dick that had fucked Ava Gardner and Lana

Turner'. Christopher Logue doesn't report on the size, so we must assume there was nothing special to report.

Johnny Stompanato, Lana Turner's gangster boyfriend, was murdered by her daughter Cheryl. His twelve-inch cock was known as Oscar. No wonder Artie Shaw didn't measure up.

My source for this intriguing fact is the *Sunday Telegraph* (8 December 2002): a review of Susan Crosland's book on gossip, *Great Sexual Scandals: 4000 Years of Debauchery* (Robson Books, £16.95).

Artie Shaw died at the very end of 2004. He was married to Ava Gardner and Lana Turner. So they didn't just fuck him and find him wanting. And I doubt if either woman waited till her wedding night to discover the disappointment behind his fly.

When Ava Gardner died, she was a lush – once she pissed herself in Hyde Park, too pissed to walk, too pissed even to crawl. She was still beautiful.

———

– I think you should have a little silver ring through your left labia, here, so you piss on it a bit whenever you go to the toilet. And when you go to the doctor with thrush or cystitis, you have to have an internal examination. He tears off a crackly sheet of green paper and you get up on the couch. When you open your legs, he parts the lips of your fanny. And sees the silver ring, about the size of a sixpence. The ring in the labia means that you have to suck off anyone who sees it. So he takes out his cock. All this in silence. Nobody speaks. Nobody needs to speak. It's understood. And it is already getting stiff. When it is completely stiff so you can see all the veins, you have to pull back his very tight foreskin, so you can see his shiny cock end, with quite a big slit in the urethra. You turn your head and get up on one elbow so you can suck his cock properly. And he comes. And you have to swallow his slightly acrid yellow spunk. Then he puts his cock away and conducts the examination, touching your clitoris and squeezing KY with a wet fart on to his rubber gloves.

– Yes. Go on. Jadwiga's mouth was tense, then it opened. As if it were forced.

– If you have two rings, one in each labia, anyone who sees them can fuck you, either in your cunt or up your arse. And after they've come, you have to suck their cocks clean.

– My shit on their cocks. It was very difficult for Jadwiga to speak. She was wanking herself.

And she came. Twice. Rysiek came inside her, unable to resist the long squeeze of her sphincter.

– And then the doctor asks about allergies and scribbles you a prescription for antibiotics (amoxicillin) and Canesten cream. But the chemist can't read his handwriting, so you have to go back …

They both laughed.

– No. That's enough. Don't touch me any more. *No.*

A day later Jadwiga told Rysiek that, shameless as she was, she was shocked to find how much she was excited by this fantasy.

– My curve is a learning curve, he said.

– What did it learn yesterday, then, you conceited man? was Jadwiga's pert rejoinder.

First sex, early-twenties sex, has all the physicality, all the strenuous overacting, of *silent film*.

Then couples find themselves *in the talkies*.

One Thousand and One Nights: Scheherazade's narratives pretend to aporia, to tantalus. The king can't kill her because he needs to know what will happen next. But the *Arabian Nights* is all about novelty, about a new woman every night, about the need for sexual excitement. (The naked narrative alibi is that the king will sleep only with virgins – the least exciting sexual option – to ensure fidelity. It can be discounted.) Scheherazade's stories are surely a synecdoche for sexual arousal – the telling of sexual fantasies, the endless excitement. A bottomless ditch of filth and fantasy. Every man his own novelist keeping his cock awake. Every woman.

Yes. Go on.

In Billy Wilder's brilliant script for *The Apartment*, with Jack Lemmon and Shirley MacLaine, C. C. Baxter (the Lemmon Nebbich character) brings a pick-up back to his apartment. She is the merest walk-on part, a plot feint, on screen for hardly four minutes. But Wilder bestows on her an 'unnecessarily' brilliant back story, a biography with no narrative relevance. It doesn't advance the plot a millimetre. She has a husband in jail in Cuba. He is a jockey who hardly weighs more than a chihuahua. Before she is expelled from the movie forever, Wilder lets her break a fingernail getting ice out of the ice-box. It isn't much and it is profligate.

Just the right amount of unnecessary detail is the guarantee of verisimilitude, of conviction, in the sexual fantasy. Not too much, certainly not too little. The conception, of course, is essential, as Matthew Arnold knew when he praised the architectonic power in the 1853 Preface to his *Poems*. But the devil is in the detail. Detail is piquant. Detail is hot.

Even when it isn't.

Especially when it isn't.

Otherwise, what? Body parts – his body part in her body part, their body parts in her body parts. Like conjugating a verb, or declining a noun. The basic grammar of sex – short of syntax, shorn of art.

———

I was having supper with Paul and Penelope Levy on 21 July 2001. The guest next to me was Anne Smith, the wife of David Smith, a schoolmaster at Marlborough, who was about to take up another teaching post at Charterhouse.

An interesting couple, who shared the same small aquiline nose. They looked like brother and sister. This is because married couples do not begin to look like each other after a lifetime together. Actually, they looked like each other all the time – right from the beginning. We are fundamentally narcissistic when it comes to love. When it comes to love, we like what we know.

Her job was to teach deaf people how to speak – deaf people who had formerly used only sign language. In *The Language*

Instinct, Steven Pinker argues that, in the acquisition of any language, timing is crucial. One example is signing used by deaf people. This system, says Pinker, is woefully maladroit if acquired late in life – but wonderfully fluent and nuanced if acquired at the early, optimum time for language learning. That is, when the window is fully open between the ages of two and three years old.

When I floated these ideas, Anne Smith said that she had only glanced at Pinker's book, but nevertheless she thought him wrong. She was aware that her views were politically unacceptable, yet her observation of signing told her that language was not a neutral instrument of communication, capable of being used clumsily or adeptly.

Theoretically, however, this must be the case – as all good writers are aware. The language we acquire will write for us, and good writing is the endless struggle towards self-consciousness – to write the language rather than be written by it. Automatism is the enemy.

But *practically* she is correct. Because a crude language will bring with it crude attitudes. Early acquisition of sign language may entail fluency and speed but it will be incapable of expressing subtleties – until it has been refined by generations and several geniuses. Language is never a neutral instrument.

Signing, in particular, looks absurdly unrefined to an outsider – especially if you are the author of a play at a signed performance. Anne Smith's job was to teach deaf people tone, nuance, tact, refinement, shading, subtlety. An example: the deaf person who has to write a letter of condolence. It begins: 'Dear X, I will tell you a joke. [Joke follows.] Now you are happy. Signature.' The content of this letter is dictated by the language of signing, which has no way of saying that, although the pain of loss is acute now, grief must have its term. The perceptions of deaf people are, therefore, impoverished, budget, unrefined.

Or merely unsentimental? Consider the sentence 'although the pain of loss is acute now, grief must have its term.' It appears subtler than telling a joke, but it is automatic, reflex, and partly a quotation from Shakespeare.

Still, there is something dismaying in the idea that local laughter at a joke might cure a deeper unhappiness.

A great writer, Joyce, has his mourners enjoying a joke in 'Hades'. But Joyce knows three things. First, that the mourners of Paddy Dignam don't really care about his death. They are merely observing custom. Secondly, that their enjoyment of a joke is realistic. Thirdly, that their enjoyment is semi-surreptitious and socially transgressive. The status of the joke is weighed, considered, subtle.

Ralf Little, the actor, showed me the sign for 'cunt' when he was acting in *Presences* at the Royal Court. Joining his thumbs and index fingers, he made a kite and situated it at his crotch. When the England football manager Sven-Göran Eriksson was being pursued by the newspapers in 2002 over his alleged affair with Ulrika Jonsson, the *Daily Mail* published on 23 April a photograph of him sitting astride a phallic bar-stool, a kind of padded mushroom. Just above the top of the stool, his hands made the kite shape – fingers down, thumbs up.

Apart from the picture editor, who else noticed? The crudity was quite subtle.

Are there no advantages to being deaf? A cruder world, perhaps, but also a more candid world?

Think of sexual silence. Think how subtle it can be in its instrumentality. Now think how terrible it can be when it is deafness. Think how direct signing would be – how unambiguous.

———

When you write a book, you let a few trusted friends see it in advance, hoping to have vulnerabilities and flaws pointed out before publication – vulnerabilities that can be protected, flaws that can be corrected. One person – who shall be strategically nameless – warned that I would be accused of name-dropping. Most readers wouldn't know that many of my friends have been patting me on the back and stabbing me in the back – as is the way with friends – for over thirty years. Another reader commented that the difficulty wouldn't arise were I as famous as my famous friends. 'If you'd won the Nobel Prize,' she said (or he said), 'the difficulty wouldn't arise.'

So I wonder if the Nobel committee can't see its collective way to solving my difficulty. Come on, Per, come on, Ingmar, we go back a long way.

———

Remember the wet fart from the tube of KY?

We all know, from personal experience, what a wet fart is. Remember? Thank God.

I can still see the eleven-year-old Rex's enriched Aertex underpants. One of an obligatory set of six – from Swinburne's, the school outfitter – they contained his wet fart. That is, they contained the recipe for his mother's fruit cake (sultanas, raisins, glacé cherries, mixed peel, lemon rind, ground almonds) in a Brown Windsor soup – by now no longer liquid, but caked after four days in his tuck locker. Ironically enough.

The Aertex underpants were twisted tightly to make rusty, perforated parentheses, folds, tucks, a pleated parcel. Strudel.

In Russia, there is a type of bread baked specially for sewer workers. It has a baked handle you throw away. A hoop, in French *calèche*. Which is why it is called a *calatch* in *Dead Souls*.

Why didn't Rex throw them away? He was a scholarship boy from the working class. He was too aware of his poverty, too aware of what it had cost his mother to buy the items on the school clothing list.

Why didn't he wash them? For two reasons. The school had no private bathrooms. He would have been seen by someone. And anyway, he couldn't have washed them clean enough to make them pass muster on linen day. The strategy he evolved was different. Smuggle the underpants in.

There was a complication. Rex couldn't be there himself. He had to be in church. Burrows had to be trusted. Confide in Burrows, the boy on linen duty.

———

Paul Steinberg's posthumous Auschwitz memoir, *Speak You Also*, is in some ways a response to Primo Levi's *If This Is a Man*, where Steinberg appears peripherally with a touch of unspecified distaste. Hence the *Also* in Steinberg's title. Levi is a morally unsleeping, morally alert writer whose power lies in his ability to bring into focus a milieu without morality. For example, there is a telling moment when the thirsty Levi asks a German guard why he has snatched away an icicle – and is told *Hier ist kein Warum*. Levi's temperament is reflective and emblematic. He is a chemist who wants to make sense of senseless Auschwitz. His mode is analytic and generalised: typically, he will talk about 'a man', or 'we', or 'the *häftling*'. It is first-hand, of course, but impersonal. He is a man whose moral instinct is uncontaminated – and he uses it to condemn his captors. A good man, he does not find himself wanting. But he finds Steinberg incomplete, lacking something, in the struggle to survive.

Steinberg is truer to the senseless Surrealism of the concentration camp experience. Morality is an avowed irrelevance for Steinberg in Auschwitz – a luxury for later. He is all pragmatism and calculation. Whereas Levi is attentive to what ought to be the case, Steinberg concentrates on what is the case. He is ruefully Nietzschean.

So, except when he ruminates about Levi and the process of writing, his experience is an unedited narrative. Including one moment when he slaps the face of an old Polish Jew who is too sick to leave his bunk. It takes immense moral courage to confess an action you have been ashamed of for fifty years. You can see the narrative equivocate, palter and finally find the truth.

He tells us that he pulls his hand away at the last second so he only grazes the old man's cheek. He tells us that at this moment he came close to joining the abyss. Then he tells us he slapped the old man. He lists the century's atrocities: 'And in this concert, I played my part.' He feels corrupted and guilty. He has fallen into the abyss, in fact. His action isn't excusable to himself. There are no extenuating circumstances as far as he is concerned. No good deed can be set against it. This one action is evil, not simply a question of pragmatic compromise.

Both Levi and Steinberg tell how you sharpen one edge of your spoon's handle so that it is also a knife. But only Steinberg tells you that being able to fart loudly was 'the prime outward sign of health that distinguishes a camp aristocrat'. It meant that your diet was superior, that you weren't suffering, as everyone else was, from chronic diarrhoea. Steinberg is the first concentration camp survivor to remember this and to mention it in his writing.

––––––––

The dirty linen at Rex's boarding school was collected every Sunday after breakfast before chapel at 10.30. It was sorted into separate heaps between the two lines of iron beds in each dormitory – grey shirts, white shirts, stiff-starched collars, grey socks, black socks, vests, underpants …

Rex always missed this ritual because he had to attend another ritual – mass at the Catholic church, St Thomas's, at 9 a.m. This was followed by a separate breakfast with his fellow Catholics and the two Jews, Baum and Coppelman. Virgo was Anglo-Irish, Anglo-Indian born in Ooty of military parents, and so blackened his baked beans with a firestorm of pepper. While the rest of the school attended chapel, the four Catholics and the two Jews lay on dormitory beds and listened to Bunk Johnson and the Firehouse Five, Humphrey Lyttelton playing 'Bad Penny Blues' on the Parlophone label, from 10.30 to 11.30.

By ten o'clock, the linen had gone. Two boys on linen duty swept each itemised heap into a separate sheet and tied its corners loosely.

But already by 9.30 the entire dormitory was hooting at Rex's underpants, which had been outed by Burrows, and Rex had a new nickname. Wet Fart.

It didn't stick, this nickname, because Rex embraced it, used it himself, found it amusing apparently, disguised his pain perfectly. And since there was no pain visible, or invisible, the boys dropped the nickname after three or four weeks.

But Burrows became known as Bunny because of his buck teeth – because it was obvious he minded.

———

On her 38th birthday the actress Olga Kempel, who was 'resting' and had been for six months, enrolled for tango lessons she could ill afford, as an indirect route to the man she loved.

There was a thirty-year age difference. He was 68, a successful playwright and allegedly a tango enthusiast. Every newspaper profile she had ever read – and her prolonged period of 'resting' left her time to explore the internet – began by mentioning his 'fatal' introduction to the tango by Jeanne Morceau, the notorious 'Crumb', long dead but seductive into her eighties. Jeanne was 70 when she seduced him as a young man of 28. Tango was his encoded, by now superstitiously compulsory, reference to her sexual charms.

They were memorable, those charms. After she had excused herself, she told him to go to the lavatory himself, before they left for the theatre to see Sartre's *Huis clos*. In the bowl, unflushed, was her powerfully scented urine. A throb of dark sunlight. A pulse. A pulse on his retina. There was no crumpled butterfly of paper improbably perched on the porcelain.

'I didn't wipe myself,' she said, unsmiling, her famous turbot lips more down-turned than usual.

She was cradling her big breasts in her folded arms like a set of twins.

'Did you piss in my piss?'

'I couldn't piss.'

'Your cock was too hard?' It wasn't really a question. He nodded.

So he introduced the tango into every interview, usually by asking the journalist if she was a tanguero. The journalists were frequently, if not invariably, female. He was very good-looking and not just for his age. His closely cut beard was pepper and salt, his eyebrows still dark, his features straight, his attentive eyes the colour of caramels, and his French accented like Omar Sharif. Without a mendacious reference to tango, he felt disloyal to the Crumb, as if he were not living in existential truth.

But he had never danced the tango.

Moreover, he was beginning to put on weight, even though he smoked so much you could hear the slight breathlessness and the sibilant rustle in his voice. A friend, the young novelist who wrote *Je suis voleur* (the successor to *Délice* which had failed in the States but haphazardly succeeded in Italy), pointed out that the pack carried a warning: smoking was the cause of impotence. (He was a non-smoker – uncensorious but pleased with himself.)

The playwright considered the warning, inhaled. 'Not my problem.'

(The young novelist assumed therefore that the old play-wright was impotent. *Therefore?* The novelist's imagination was young, if not exactly innocent. But the playwright's problem was priapism – the amount of time he wasted when he could have been writing.)

'My problem is weight. I don't know how it is. I weigh more than I've ever weighed in my life. I smoke so I depress my appetite. I eat hardly anything. I drink nothing. OK, there are all these lunches' – they were having lunch, outside – 'but I never have a starter, or a pudding. Fuck it, I will have a pudding. I don't care. Well, I do, but fuck it all the same.'

And he ordered the sour cherries in mascarpone.

He wasn't very fat but his waist-line had begun to look comfortable. And he had hated a recent photograph in the 'Culture' section of *Le Monde*. He thought his unstructured linen suit made him look like Babar. As if he were a paper model someone had crumpled up, then tried to straighten out. As a young man, he had favoured high-waisted, tight military trousers with a sabre stripe from ribcage to stirrup instep. Impossible now. Possibly impossible forever.

(Unless, of course, he contracted lung cancer. With its secondary slimming effect. He lit another Gitanes. And extinguished it almost immediately.)

———

Olga had loved him for two years and spoken to him twice – once in the cafeteria of the Théâtre Racine, where he was rehearsing *C'est tu, Albert?* on the main stage. She was in another play by him in one of the rehearsal rooms just off rue Monsieur le Prince. The theatre was putting on a season of his plays. Her table was in the smoking section and it had a place free. All the other smoking tables were taken.

'May I?'

'Sure.' She had her lighter ready. A white crocus of flame, a sway of pollen. She didn't smoke. Things were going to plan. She had turned other people away, saying the seat was for a friend.

'I'm Sarah in *Ulysse*.'

'You must be …'

'Olga Kempel.'

'Right. Olga Kempel.' He smiled. 'How's it coming, Olga Kempel?'

'Pretty good. It's a neat little play. I love it. And you write good women's parts.'

'So they say. But they also say, don't they, that my men are joke machines?'

'Quite a good idea in comedy, I'd say.'

'I think you might be too intelligent to be an actress. Not many people get the, you know, crucial symbiosis there, here in post-Heideggerian France. You must be a real handful. To direct, I mean.' He was flirting automatically, applying the warm oil. The pause between 'handful' and 'to direct' was purely professional – the playwright, the director at work. *Could you just try a little pause, fractional, less than a beat? Good.*

'We're still improvising. Exercises and impro.'

'And you want to get on to the text? Well, it *is* brilliantly written.' She was quite good-looking, he thought, beginning to engage.

Olga had a useful face for an actress. It wasn't conventionally pretty, but it was striking and animated when she talked. Her jaw and her aquiline nose weren't small. Her lips were fine and faintly humorous. She wasn't plain but she could play a plain person on stage convincingly. She could make herself read as beautiful or as ugly, though she was neither. Her hair was glorious, a thick dull chestnut, wavy as a picture frame, and her eyelashes an intense ochre. Across her nose a banner of burnt sequins. Her flaw was something tinny in her vocal range. Which meant that she would never be out of work but she couldn't play leads. At drama school, her best friend had a prognathous jaw and piano legs. She got all the servant parts, what she called the Bessy parts.

'You know the Peter Brook story?' she asked.

'The one with Gielgud?'

'Yea. It's great, isn't it?'

'I want you to *terrify* me.'

They spoke in unison: '*We open in two weeks.*' And laughed. Her teeth were good. His were too small for his mouth; so, childish and oddly touching.

'It's true, though. Brook prefers rehearsal, the process, all that. If he could just ditch the text, he'd be happy. Approximate narration, he'd be fine with that.'

And with that, the playwright got to his feet, ground out his cigarette and said, 'Very nice meeting you, Olga Kempel.'

He waved at someone across the cafeteria, then sat down to chat for a few minutes to the very pretty designer who was in for the morning. No leg warmers for her. Scarlet fingernails like a Calder mobile.

Olga couldn't judge how much she had registered with him, but she liked the way he used her full name, as if he were trying to fix it in his database.

———

The second occasion was shorter, but more significant. It was at the party after the opening of *Ulysse*. The playwright was pushing his way past her through the crowd, holding up a bouquet of five champagne flutes, dangerously angled. His cigarette danced in his lips as he said, 'Olga Kempel, you were very good.' At first she thought he was winking, but he was trying to keep the smoke out of his eye.

He had remembered her name.

———

She was a happy woman for the rest of the three-week run – always expecting to bump into him backstage or front of house or in the crush bar afterwards. But it was the Brook version of *Waiting for Godot*. The central non-appearance retained and all the other details improvised nightly.

Six months later she decided to take up the tango. She might meet him at one of those milongas on the granite steps of Saint-Sulpice or the marble foyer of the Gare du Nord.

———

'Maybe I should just forget about him. Get another fella, Émilie. What do you think?'

She was with another actress friend. They were on their fourth Caipirinha. It was one in the morning.

Émilie yawned. 'Did I tell you I had this tremendous crush on Pierre le Roux when we did that lousy *Andromaque* at the Bouffe du Sud? Why am I yawning?' She looked at her watch. 'It's only one o'clock. Anyway, I was completely obsessed. Something to do with his aloofness. You know how fucking aloof he is. I just thought, he has to fucking realise. Has to. It's so fucking *obvious*. I was like this fucking schoolgirl.' She put on the face of a blinking ingénue. 'I mean, I was walking rapid-eye movement. In a fucking dream. I was. A somnabulist in the cafeteria.'

She bent to suck the straw in her drink.

'So one night, right at the end of the run, we were on the same train to Meudon. And I thought, now or never. I must speak. So just before his stop, I said, there's something I have to tell you. His back was to me because he was getting his coat and a valise down from the luggage rack. I couldn't have said it to his face. So I said, I'm just in love with you.'

'What did he say?'

'He said. He said, O Christ, not again. And I burst into tears. And he said, Look I'm sorry, I really am, but this is my stop. Clamart. And that was that. For the last three performances, he kept as far away as possible.'

The two actresses burst out laughing and ordered another pair of Caipirinhas.

At three o'clock, Émilie said, 'But you have to tell him. Otherwise he might never know, you know?'

———

So Olga wrote him a note, inviting him to lunch at the Café Flore. On her. He couldn't make it. He was in London that week talking to Richard Eyre at the National about his new play, *Bonjour, Venise*. An unsuccessful meeting, as it turned out. Then he was in final rehearsals at Rio.

She suggested another date. And this time he accepted. He thought she was looking for work and that he might cast her as part of the replacement cast of *Bonjour, Venise* when it transferred. If it transferred. The producer was finding the finding of a theatre inexplicably hard. Nothing was free for the period they needed and the actors were committed to other projects outside the time-frame specified in their contracts.

Sounding more like Omar Sharif than ever and concentrating his dark chocolate eyes, he suggested that, though nothing in theatre could ever be relied on, she might like the little part of Suzette – if the bloody thing ever transferred.

'You know,' he confided, 'we are part of a profession where your heart is broken twice weekly.'

Olga agreed. And she agreed to take the part.

'So you didn't tell him you were crazy about him?'

'Émilie, he offered me a part. That must mean something.'

'Yes. He thinks you can act. He's seen you act. You can act. You're bloody good with that reedy little voice of yours.' And she did the reedy voice.

'But he must like me. Don't you think? He could choose a million actresses.'

'Yea and he asked you. No, that is a good sign. It just isn't conclusive. Your turn to buy the drinks.'

'Shall we start a tab?'

'Yea, OK.'

They were drinking Margaritas. A crushed necklace of salt on the rim of the glasses.

Someone was singing (rather brilliantly) 'New York, New York' at the karaoke. Belting it out in English. Everyone joined in for the last chorus.

'Do you think he's already got a girlfriend? He must have a girlfriend. Émilie?'

'Why must? He's not so young any more. Did you see that photograph in *Le Monde*? He's definitely put on weight. Sorry.'

'I think he's having an affair with that designer.'

'Who? The Arvon lady. Come on, he's got better taste than that.'

'Yes,' Olga said. 'She is a bit cosmetics counter. But she designs all his shows. And she's single.'

'Isn't she supposed to be lesbian?'

'No, she was married to that Lloyd's Name, chap at the Bourse, what's his name?'

'So? I heard she was lesbian.'

'Well, maybe she isn't any more. And wasn't there a rumour that he was shagging horse-face, the one who's married to Jonty Steele? She was in *C'est tu, Albert?* The first time round. She went with it to New York. He was there right through rehearsals.'

The rest of the evening was spent casting the playwright's possible lovers. There were many, many plausible candidates and all of them seemed available to Olga.

She didn't realise that several well-informed intimates of the playwright were certain that *she* was the playwright's secret significant other. Émilie wasn't the only actress friend she'd talked to. Somehow, frustration and tantalus had been transfigured by gossip into their opposites – fulfilment and closure.

––––––––

In the end, she asked him. They were having a drink – to console him for the failure of *Bonjour, Venise* to find a suitable theatre in Paris, and to console her for the loss of the part.

'Would you like to tango later?' Olga said. 'There's a milonga apparently at the Tuileries. Good dancing surface just where the pyramid ...'

He interrupted. 'If I tell you something, would you promise ...'

'Soul of discretion. Scouts' honour.'

He shook his head. His fingers played a scale on the thick nap of his new young buzz-cut. Up. Down. 'No. I can't. Not even with you.'

Not even with you.

He meant – it was almost an aside to himself – that it wouldn't matter if she were disappointed, surprised or shocked to learn that his tango technique was a lie.

Olga took it differently. She was special.

'Are you in love with someone?'

He was surprised by the change of direction, but addressed this new topic.

'In a way, yes. In a way.'

'How do you mean, in a way?'

'All right, just "yes".'

'Do I know her, the person you're in love with?' Olga was expecting the answer, yes, *you*.

He smiled and turned his cigarette packet on the marble table top as if he were boxing a compass. Where were they exactly?

'No,' he said. 'You don't know her. She's Russian. An émigré. I met her at a party.'

'Does she have a name?' Olga felt her voice get reedier.

'Larissa. Like Lara in *Doctor Zhivago*.' He smiled, sounding even more like Omar Sharif.

'Is she very beautiful?' Olga asked.

'I think so,' he said. 'But these things are subjective.'

'And she's very young?' It was hardly a question.

He laughed. 'She's younger than me. Just a bit.'

Olga thought he was being ironic – that 'just a bit' meant 'at least thirty years'. Not for the first time, she was wrong.

Why did the playwright choose the 61-year-old Larissa when he could have slept with the much younger Olga? Or any of a hundred nubile actresses? Was it because he thought her gratitude would outweigh his physical shortcomings? His fatness?

His age? Perhaps his penis was small? Larissa said it was fine – a big one. But she is inexperienced. However, she is correct in this case.

I think you know why he wanted the Russian. Why he preferred her to anyone else, including Olga Kempel.

He preferred older women.

Especially when they happened to look at him through the eyes of Jeanne Morceau. Even if the expression in those eyes was laughably inexperienced.

So there would be the additional pleasure of corrupting her profound innocence – the pleasure for her, as well as for him.

————

Piotr's affair with Agnieszka came to an end one day when he discovered the tumour on the underside of his scrotum. Though it was difficult to see, it already felt sizeable, though painless. Painless at first. Piotr began to experience sudden pangs, acute piercings, worse than a wasp sting, which stopped him in the street. The site of the tumour coincided with the crossroads of seams in the crotch of his Levi 501s. That design flaw where the seams start playing sandwiches. Club sandwiches.

He definitely felt like a mayfly. But the thought of his imminent extinction, now so real and proximate, took away his sexual desire. Particularly since the threat to his existence was situated in his genitals. It was as if *they*, the genitals, were themselves responsible. Without his scrotum, Piotr would be hale, happily sexless, ordering drinks in a bar, with a future before him. Sex didn't seem so important.

There is a risible moment at the end of Hemingway's *A Farewell to Arms*, when Hemingway imagines his dying heroine putting this ridiculous request of her lover, Frederic Henry, a character without a proper surname: 'You won't do our things with other women, will you?' The egotistic male point of view. In death, the female thoughtfully finds space to worry about the future of our penis.

In the *Guardian* (2 September 2002) Nigella Lawson was interviewed. The journalist asked if her dead husband wanted her to re-marry after his death. She gave a qualified answer that shows how intelligent she is: 'Yes. But when you're dying you're not really thinking about what comes after.'

This is why Hemingway's close to *A Farewell to Arms* is just wrong. What we see there is a human truth in disguised form. Hemingway's failure of imagination *is* a failure but it also inadvertently discloses a truth. Which is this: we are egotists at all times. Even when someone we love is dying. Frederic Henry is 100 per cent absorbed in the death of his wife – except for the 1 per cent which is already imagining the future. The dying Catherine is egotistical, too – fair enough – we know that all she is thinking about is her own death, that she has no time for altruism or jealousy.

———

In March 2001, on the ski-bus from my hotel to the Kaprun ski-lift, I encountered one of life's great truths. Let me share it with you. This principle is called *The cut on someone else's finger*.

Three Germans, clearly friends, sat across the aisle – two of them facing a third. Their conversation was animated without being argumentative. As you know, the crucial thing about skis is their edge. The inside edge has to be sharp, otherwise turning is difficult, especially on ice. You may have noticed that ice skaters protect their blades – their *blades* – with sheaths. Same principle. All three Germans had their skis between their legs, holding them in the middle, near the bindings, at the sharpest point. Suddenly, one of them gasped. *Scheisse.* There were gouts of blood the size of redcurrants on his finger. The others looked, tut-tutted, *and went on with their conversation.* The injured German took no further part in the discussion. He was staring at the island of blood seeping through his handkerchief.

I was reminded of this later in the year at Spoleto, where I was giving a poetry reading as part of the festival. At the final concert, there were two thousand people in the piazza in front of the cathedral's Romanesque façade. Rai Due TV cameras on booms swooped, then soared away like the swifts overhead. Richard Hickox conducted and perspired fluently. There was a choir of nearly a hundred. There was also a woman having a heart attack quite near the front, approximately in Row D. Around her, a little eddy of chaos. Someone was pounding her chest – an improvised version of a defibrillator. Others whispered intensely into their mobile phones. Her legs were raised. You could see where her tights darkened at the upper thigh as they modulated into the more robust panty section. A cardinal at the edge of the proceedings, acting urgency, paced and turned in his dramatic clericals with the strange, camp air of someone modelling Vivienne Westwood. Paramedics, a nurse, a stretcher appeared. The heart attack victim was tidied away – and the concert continued.

In fact, the concert had never stopped. For perhaps fifteen minutes, a considerable section of the audience – the hundred or so with a reasonable view – was distracted from the concert. Now they refocused their attention to the stage. *The cut on someone else's finger.*

I thought of Jane Austen – who drily remarked after a battle, 'What a tragedy so many fine young men were killed and what a blessing we cared for none of them.'

————

Let me describe the tumour on Piotr's scrotum. With the aid of a small hand mirror and an anglepoise lamp, he was able to see his arsehole, its crow's-feet, its café au lait colour, touched with notes of iodine and espresso, his anal hairs. No picnic area. He could also get a fix on the tumour – if a tremulous, hand-held one – when he held his testicles out of the way. It was the size of a large lentil, yellow under the skin. Its texture was hard and initially painless for most of the time. Over the weeks, it slightly but inexorably increased in mass and formed a kind of peak so that it resembled a large thorn under the skin. It was at this stage that it was capable of stopping him in the street as it snagged on his jeans. He began to wear his jeans slung fashionably low. It was still painful.

He was too shy and too fatalistic to see a doctor.

He was too shy to show the tumour to Agnieszka. Or to tell her that he had reached the terrible predicted point in Ecclesiastes when desire fails.

Or that, in the circumstances, he wanted his wife and his three children more than her. (Not that he mentioned his problem to Basia.)

So he broke off with Agnieszka without an explanation, leaving on her answerphone a long, rambling message of regret, resolve, but no clarity. Which she broadcast at intervals through loud speakers at the party she threw for her feminist friends. She was angry and vengeful.

The next day, hungover, she took refuge in poetry. She wrote furiously for several months.

As we shall see.

For five years Piotr never saw her again.

––––––––––

Maybe Piotr should have let Agnieszka see the site of his trauma. After all, he and she were very frank, very vocal, in bed. There is a difference. Not all candour is the same. Candour is plural. Sexual candour was easy for both – as easy as it ever is. Physical candour, without the morphine of arousal, was impossible for Piotr.

Whereas women seem to be habituated to opening their legs – to doctors, to nurses, to midwives. At least *some* women appear phlegmatic, wryly resigned to inspection. But, phlegmatic or not, it doesn't alter the female condition – which is one of enforced exhibitionism. A man could quite easily get through life without once exposing himself to his physician. Most do. Whereas a woman …

T. S. Eliot had a congenital hernia for which he wore a truss. It wasn't till the early forties that the rupture was surgically repaired, so it had been part of his physical reality for as long as he could remember. His first wife, Vivienne, had heavy and extended periods: she was constantly laundering sheets at hotels and homes where the couple were guests. I imagine they were too shy to have definitive, lengthy discussions about either disability.

The truss was much more common before 1940. Ruskin had his trusses made bespoke at an address in Greek Street. Matthew Arnold ironically invokes the iconic power of the Truss Manufactory behind Trafalgar Square, noting that the Irish Fenian has no instinct of appreciation for this symbolic British building. In *Sons and Lovers*, Paul Morel works as a junior spiral clerk in a factory that makes trusses and artificial limbs.

It was a large concern.

(So large, in fact, that I find myself wondering if the truss isn't the vulgar and therefore unnamed item that Mrs Newsome's vast fortune is founded on in Henry James's *The Ambassadors*. Of course, it could be the toilet brush or lavatory paper.)

Physically, the nineteenth and early-twentieth centuries were times when intimate problems were difficult to disclose straightforwardly and difficult to hide. Constance Garnett, the great Russian translator, had a prolapsed womb which was kept in place by the insertion of some mechanical device. When she was travelling the length of Russia, how did she keep it clean? How did it actually work? Could she keep it a secret? Certainly, it affected her sex life. She was given to Platonic pashes and she was tolerant of her husband's sexual compensations outside the marriage. Embarrassment is a powerful human emotion, capable of overturning Victorian sexual mores.

It is possible, too, that Harriet Mill, whose second husband was J. S. Mill, had a *mariage blanc* on the second occasion, though her first marriage produced three children – and, it is likely, a prolapsed womb, for which the standard euphemism at the time was 'back problems'. Mill's *Autobiography* doesn't suggest a husband capable of coming to an accommodation other than affectionate celibacy.

These last two cases, of Constance Garnett and Harriet Mill, are exemplary. Though not in quite the way you might imagine at first glance. In each case, a prolapse rules out sexual intercourse, it seems. And that is that. But what about the h-j in HJ? What about the hand-job in Henry James's *Wings of the Dove*? Merton Densher and Kate Croy cannot afford to marry, for financial, worldly reasons, but their creator is himself worldly enough to suggest a remedy and a relief. His and their strategic surrogate isn't explicit, of course. How could it be? It is virtually invisible in the 1902 first edition – an opaque suggestion. But in the 1909 New York edition James comes clean – and is, therefore, dirtier, though you need to be a lawyer, inured to small print, to see it. (It was pointed out to me by Alison Macdonald, a barrister at Matrix Chambers.)

The full quote is to be found in Book 6, Chapter 1 (or Chapter 17): 'He had known more than ever, on their separating in the court of the station, how ill a man, and even a woman, could feel from such a cause; but he struck himself as also knowing that he had already suffered Kate to begin finely [my edition stops here, and adds 'to manipulate it'] to apply antidotes and remedies and subtle sedatives.'

So, what about masturbation, fellatio, cunnilingus, inter-femural intercourse, sodomy – all the skills that flesh is heir to? Think of Monica Lewinsky. Surely the Mills and the Garnetts – though Victorians, Edwardians – were as alert as a White House intern to these obvious stratagems? Apparently not. From which I deduce, consulting my own representative maleness, that the disgust is self-disgust on the woman's part, not disgust on the man's. All those surrogates seem acceptable to my average maleness. (And on occasion, preferable – not just surrogates.) Physical embarrassment, it seems, cancels the sexual in every manifestation. Which may seem unlikely. Until you consider the smell of Mrs Garnett's device and how she might feel.

And especially how she might feel when she menstruated. You might find it hard to be phlegmatic about that, except on your own.

Consider an embarrassing, purely male affliction – the hydro-cele. A hydrocele is a swelling of the testicle caused by a leaking of fluid from the prostate. Coleridge had a hydrocele. So did Dr Johnson (he writes memorably about the *shiny* sur-face of his scrotum). So did an acquaintance of mine. Ten years previously, when his left testicle became the size of a cricket ball, he went to his GP, who pronounced it a hydrocele. There were two methods of treatment: a syringe in the testicle once a month to draw off the fluid; or an operation. Naturally, my friend opted for the syringe. This proved to be so painful that he decided an operation, to repair the leak permanently, was preferable.

For a month after the operation, his scrotum – like a flayed rabbit – was sewn to his stomach.

I gave an all-male dinner party the day he told me this. We began with avocados that were overripe. I wasn't sure whether they were actually inedible and gave one to another guest, a flamboyant homosexual, who weighed it in his hand, squeezed it and announced that it was exactly like a hydrocele.

My other friend was aghast. 'You told him.' The homosexual was a notorious gossip.

'No,' I said. 'You did. Just now.'

A woman would have been less embarrassed in all-female company. After all, my friend's hydrocele was ten years previously.

But it partly explains why Piotr was so reluctant to seek a diagnosis from his doctor. There was another reason, too. The doctor was irrelevant – certainly, by now, only palliatives would be on offer, and right from the start it was already too late. Piotr knew in advance that the thing was fatal.

––––––––

You see, a superstitious part of Piotr also thought that his affliction was a site-specific punishment for infidelity.

He decided to take matters into his own hands.

That is how he came to be sitting on the edge of the sofa bed, his face glossy with sweat, his trousers round his ankles, his underpants round his calves, his testicles in his left hand. A concentrated August sun shone into the eighth-floor room. A new book of bright needles lay open on the counterpane directly catching the sunlight. When he looked away, Piotr could see their after-image.

There were ten of them. Mercurial yet single in the sun, they seemed an ideogram. A logo for the broken waterfall that falls, then fails from sight, then fails again. The brand name was Dorcas, after the dressmaker who was raised from the dead.

Piotr was afraid he might forget. But his notebook was on the tablecloth across the room, and he was shackled to the bed.

He selected the biggest needle. Bending forward, two large drops of sweat smashed on the parquet floor. His German varifocals were a problem. When he craned and angled his head to look at the tumour, the vital tiny section of lens was unavailable. He took off his spectacles. Sometimes, for very close tasks – picking splinters out of his boys' feet – he could see better without them.

The thought of his three sons, when they were small, made all nine needles contract and straighten as two tears fell to the floor.

Nor did his thickened waistline make bending easy either. He grunted down and forward, persevered, though his breathing was constricted. A vein darkened in his red neck.

But there it was. Bigger than a lentil now. Perhaps the size of a borlotti bean. He brought the point of the needle to catch on the taut glaze of the tumour. Several drops of sweat fell rapidly. He pushed in the needle half a centimetre's length. He expected pain but experienced only a mild queasy discomfort.

He had also imagined one of two outcomes. A jet of fluid and subsequent deflation. Or a seriously aggravated and accelerating aggressive tumour.

The second seemed at first the more likely outcome. When he withdrew the needle, there was barely a drop of blood. He sat up, recovered his composure, then squeezed himself down again and introduced the needle once more, fractionally to the left of the original entry point. With identical results, though the two holes visibly united under pressure from below. He could just make out dark yellow matter through the hole.

And he decided to squeeze it, hoping to induce a jet of pus and blood. What emerged, quite painfully, was no jet but a kind of solidified pus the texture of suet. Like dried ear wax, it was malleable. A friable excrement. He smeared it, experimentally, between his thumbnails.

Finally, after five minutes, the tumour was gone and a drop of dark blood appeared. He dabbed it with a clean handkerchief, applied some antiseptic cream and dressed.

Piotr kept the needles safely hidden – in case the tumour returned.

––––––––––

At the same time as Véra, after a routine mammogram, was diagnosed with pre-cancerous cells in her left breast, Rysiek received an A4-sized brown paper parcel through the post. It was Agnieszka's new sequence of poems – a detailed account of her affair with Piotr, full of persuasive circumstantial touches. She was offering them for publication by Rysiek's press.

When I wrote that she was writing furiously, it wasn't a thoughtless cliché. While there was no mention of her phantom 'cancer', following Basia's blow to her skull, the typescript was an exhaustive indictment of Piotr's deficiencies as a lover and a catalogue of his physical shortcomings.

Particularly his penis.

It wasn't a cock so much as a skin tag.

But his skin tags were the size of goujons.

Piotr was perfunctorily disguised as Petya and therefore recognisable to everyone who knew him, though not to Rysiek, who agreed to publish a small commercial edition.

––––––––––

Writers who don't raise hackles, who are admired, not envied: William Trevor, Brian Moore, V. S. Pritchett, Penelope

Fitzgerald. None of them show-boating writers. Small commercial editions, *reasonably* successful.

(Maybe critics prefer middling writers because they enhance the critic's function? The critic as shaman. Once you discount the obviously good writers – as egotists who are interposing their *writing* between the reader and the reality to be rendered – and you are left with the undistinguished and indistinguishable. Indistinguishable, that is, except by the critic, who palms off his purely subjective preferences with phantom 'analysis' of alleged, but invisible, literary effects. His professionalism, his 'expertise', allows him to arbitrate – arbitrarily.)

I once asked a family friend of William Golding what he was like. I was told he was modest, considered, contained, except for a single drunken occasion when he swung from the frame of some French windows, shouting *I'm a bloody genius.* It is better not to let people see this certainty. They do not enjoy it.

And some writers are unable to hide it. Salman Rushdie, for example, who allegedly walked out of the Booker Prize dinner when *Shame* did not win. (*If* he did.) But you would know from Rushdie's writing, from his prose, that he was confident of his talent. There is an apocryphal story about Salman – I know it is apocryphal because I heard him deny it at a dinner where it was told as a tease by Martin Amis. At a writers' conference in Finland, there is an annual football match, in which Salman scored the two winning goals – 'a power-header from fifteen yards' and 'a perfect lob after a feinted drive'. Obviously, the source for these quotations was supposed to be Salman.

Penelope Fitzgerald's letters have just been published (summer 2008). They reveal that she disliked Rushdie and also Malcolm Bradbury. I have read three reviews, by Hermione

Lee in the *Sunday Times*, by Julian Barnes in the *Guardian* and by Hilary Spurling in the *Observer*. Only Hilary Spurling understands the set-up, the artificiality of this unstudiedness.

Julian Barnes and Hermione Lee simply praise her as a remarkable talent emerging from a hyper-ordinary set of unglamorous, untidy circumstances. Hilary Spurling, though, can see that the persona is a persona.

You are the clever niece of the Knox brothers – but ignored and unsuccessful. You are a failure – so you systematically snub success. You cultivate unworldliness. But you are like Gilbert Osmond in *The Portrait of a Lady*. You are in thrall to worldly success – whose value you refuse to acknowledge. Whose values you despise and dismiss. This is your perverse tribute.

Worldly success includes Julian Barnes, though he doesn't seem to realise it. Fitzgerald simply won't accept a lift in a taxi – and, in his version, goes to ingenious lengths to thwart his charitable offer. He doesn't understand why. Rather than accept a taxi ride, the discomfort of the tube is preferable because it allows her not to acknowledge the existence of his literary success. Julian Barnes – *who remembers nothing of their conversation from York to London King's Cross* – is made invisible, too. Fitzgerald was, in other words, a poisonous failure and when success came it was too late to change her calculated manner of absent-minded superiority.

The self-servingness of self-effacement. Again.

Automatic unpopularity is interesting – the way, for instance, that Tony Blair became Tony Bliar. The way everyone on the left preferred Gordon Brown. What went wrong? Blair was too good at winning elections, too good at reforming the

Labour Party, too brilliant at the dispatch box during Prime Minister's Question Time, too clever, too confident. (All this before Iraq.)

There are many people it is safe to despise, who can be automatically despised. They share one quality – a perceived cockiness.

It is OK to despise Tony Parsons, for example. He appears on *Late Night Review* with his cockney accent and Samsonite confidence. Then he starts a successful career as a novelist.

In the *Observer Magazine* (18 August 2002) Lynn Barber interviewed him. Her piece was titled 'Meet the Parent'. She was irritated by his apparent adoption of a New Man persona. Lynn Barber used to be slim and a beauty and was clearly offended by Parsons's dislike of fat women: 'Some of the sentiments in these columns are rather strikingly at odds with his new Sensitive persona. The most notorious probably is the "Death of the White Woman" written in 1991: "Why do most men prefer – either in their lives or in their fantasies – the comfort of brown-eyed girls rather than big brood mares with dyed hair and sagging tits? Why? Are you kidding?"'

Clearly, these generalisations are fuelled by dislike of his fat ex-wife Julie Burchill.

Lynn Barber offered another explanation for this allegedly self-evident choice: '(We big brood mares always assume it's because Asian babes are more kindly disposed towards weeny peenies, but wash my laptop out with soap for making that remark).'

Later in her piece, Lynn Barber invoked Burchill directly: 'No doubt he didn't like her describing their first lovemaking in her autobiography as "nasty, brutish and short" …'

The allusion to Hobbes's *Leviathan* won't fool anyone about the important adjective there.

Is it surprising that the resentment about his cockiness should express itself in innuendo about his cock? Wordplay is like a mule, an innocent carrying contraband. (Think about the unconscious play on 'endowment' in *Humboldt's Gift*.) But what does it mean? Perhaps this: we can't overcome our ingrained, atavistic prejudice that, ultimately, confidence is based on sexual confidence. That certainty, confidence in one's powers, is finally just a form of willy-waggling. The word itself – cockiness – isn't accidentally linked. It is coined on purpose.

In the *Observer* (1 September 2002) Harriet Lane reviewed Tony Parsons's *Man and Wife*: 'Parsons deals with his large cast with all the cool professionalism of a Scandinavian football coach: setting up some tension here, easing it off a little there. The sentences are short, pithy and efficient, usually beginning with a conjunction; the paragraphs are often one line, hanging meaningfully on the page like a kid smoking at the bus stop.' The headline over the piece: 'Short, pithy and efficient. And that's just the sentences.'

Some sub at the *Observer* doesn't like Tony Parsons. But maybe it isn't so personal. Obviously, no one at the *Observer* likes Tony Parsons. He's a safe person to dislike automatically.

It was this licensed, reflex ridicule Piotr feared.

———

In the afterword to *Lolita*, Vladimir Nabokov says that 'reality' is a word that should never be used without inverted commas. Piotr hasn't read *Lolita*, though he translated *Pnin* for a

Krakow publishing house. (His fee paid for those German varifocals and a postal after-care cleansing service.) All the same, his experience supports Nabokov.

Of course, Agnieszka's poems were untrue. But they became true. Piotr's penis definitely diminished in size.

With immediate effect.

In the fifties the linguist Edward Sapir and his star student Benjamin Whorf argued that reality is a social construct, created by language. The crude basis of what became known as the Whorf-Sapir Hypothesis is that different languages condition our thinking in different ways – and therefore the way we perceive the world. Whorf and Sapir's examples were taken from the language of the Hopi Indians. (Neither man spoke Hopi.) Steven Pinker in *The Language Instinct* destroyed their theory by pointing out that their examples were translated in a way that maximised their difference from standard English. Pinker offered a counter example – the simple sentence 'He walks' – and 'translated' it as follows: 'Masculine uprightness proceeds leggedly.' Pinker also showed that thought precedes language, by means of a simple experiment designed to show that babies still unable to speak can negotiate a form of mental arithmetic. We think, says Pinker, in mentalese, his word for a pre-linguistic process. We know what it means to write something down and cross it out because it doesn't express our thought properly.

It is also true that translation would be completely impossible, given the Whorf-Sapir Hypothesis. Because Baudelaire is a French speaker, his reality differs from that of his English translator. There is no way of rendering that reality, created by the French language, into the English version of reality. But because the English translator speaks French – let us say he is bilingual – he has two versions of reality from which to choose. (Not a state of affairs translators ever draw to our attention.) Nevertheless, he has to *choose* between these competing and *parallel* realities.

The Whorf-Sapir theory was once powerful in literary theoretical circles – powerful because it implicitly subverted the conservative idea of an unchangeable reality and was an implicit argument for relativity and political radicalism. It is now completely discredited.

Except with Piotr, the unwitting proselyte, who became an example of language's power to reorganise reality, of art's ability to alter the human condition. Piotr's poor prick was living proof.

If it seemed small, foreshortened, when he gazed down at it, did it look larger in the mirror? Aren't our reflections subtly smaller than reality? So that, in fact, it was larger than it looked?

He looked up the average size of the erect human penis. (A measure that varied, depending on the source. Obviously. It is bound to be approximate. How big is the sample? Is the sample self-selecting – with the big penises eager, vocal, proactive, while the tiny penises boycott the project? What is the statistical margin of error? Who measures the sample? The subject? Is self-service self-serving?)

Whatever.

But he knew that the median meant penises both larger and smaller, which were averaged out. Someone had to be under the cut-off line.

And where do you measure from? From the tip to the top of

the pubic tuft? Or along the longer underside? If the latter, where is it generally agreed that the penis stops, since it seems to reach back to the perineum? If your penis is curved (Piotr was like Rysiek: see his ready erection on p. 29), a ruler is less flattering than a tape measure or a piece of string. The ruler measures only the length of the bow from end to end, not the *actual* length. A ruler measures as the crow flies, the quickest route because the *shortest* route.

The answer to the question 'How long is a piece of string?' is 'Longer.'

He thought he remembered an earlier time when his erect penis reached almost to his navel. It seemed much further off now. But if he bent his spine and sank in his stomach, he could bring the tip closer. Perhaps that was his naturally concentrated wanking position in adolescence – before he became so laid back about the whole sex thing …

He was trying to recall what Kristina, the first old girlfriend, had said about his cock years ago. She was a very experienced woman. They were talking about Zbigniew's cock. Zbigniew was a computer wonk with, according to Kristina, the largest cock she'd ever sucked. And mine? Piotr asked in those long-lost sexually confident days. She answered with a Moroccan proverb, spoken with a guttural lilt, a comic foreign accent. *Short and fat pleases wife and makes good baby.* He was content with that answer.

Short? *Short?* Of course, you wouldn't want a long penis, would you, if it was long because it was thin? Fat. Fat was good. And he remembered that Kristina had wanted to marry him.

He also remembered Jurek in the school lavatories, the way his huge flaccid prick became hard without increasing its width or its length. Well, it hardly needed to. Nevertheless, there was comfort to be gleaned from Jurek. He was an argument towards a democracy of dimensions. The smaller penis when erect underwent a complete makeover. It surpassed itself.

Piotr's main problem was the penis unerect. *The* penis? His penis. Of course, everyone's penis exhibits a variety of states. The trouble with the penis unerect is that this fluctuating state happens to include the smallest manifestation. And that, increasingly, was the shrunken state sheltering in the oubliette of his lightless underpants.

(*Increasingly*. Very funny, thinks Piotr.)

———

When Michael Ondaatje's novel *The English Patient* was published in 1992, it was reviewed by Nicholas Spice in the *London Review of Books* (24 September 1992, Volume14, Number18, pp. 3–5). Spice's first sentence attacked a sentence on the first page. The penis of the 'English Patient', Almasy, is said to sleep like a sea-horse. He has been badly burned. Spice could not see the justice of the simile. Why is a raven like a writing desk? 'Can a penis sleep like a sea horse?'

Why *is* a penis curled like a sea-horse? Of course, in many ways, a penis doesn't resemble a sea-horse. That is the point of metaphor. If the tenor and the vehicle are identical, the metaphor is a dud. There has to be a dissimilarity that is over-ridden by the justice of the similarity.

I infer that Count Almasy's penis is uncircumcised, and at its smallest seems all foreskin, so that the shrivelled prepuce is the length of the sea-horse's crinkle-cut tail. Ondaatje's sentence – 'his penis was sleeping like a sea-horse' – uses 'sleeping' as a kindly euphemism for 'curled up' and decidedly defunct.

It was this state of affairs that Piotr so disliked. The smallest state.

———

After a couple of miserable months, following the publication of Agnieszka's chapbook, Piotr sent his expensive *Pnin* spectacles back to Bavaria for a service. The protective coating on the lenses was beginning to flake and cloud. For a month he was forced to wear his old pair of Polish spectacles with their superseded prescription. The nose pieces left deep dints. Worse: wearing them, his cock looked even smaller. Paradoxically, it was at once fuzzier and smaller. Neither were they flattering to his increasingly morose features.

Finally, the sparkling varifocals were returned retuned.

And everything looked bigger. *Everything*. The books on his bookshelves increased in size. Not much. But enough. B-format trade paperbacks became demy octavo. And his cock looked fine. A thing of substance.

The phenomenon lasted a whole Thursday before his vision accustomed itself to the refurbished glasses with their new prescription.

By Friday everything had returned to abnormal.

Cognitive dissonance was back, distorting his self-perception.

Sexual confidence is evanescent – easily lost and recovered only with difficulty.

As I know. As you know. As we know.

It would have been useless to tell Piotr an obvious truth: that women have left men for other men with smaller penises. He was incapable of re-configuring Agnieszka's narrative.

———

Ten, twenty years ago, Professor Ray Dolan administered sodium pentothal to English patients with disabilities like blindness and paralysis that were caused by hysteria. There was no physical basis for their various handicaps. He then filmed them, sighted and walking. The patients were shown the film. The result was not cure, as you might expect. They simply re-configured their stories.

Piotr was a tiny bit mad. But not mad enough to be able to re-write her poems.

———

With the advent of Véra's cancer, Rysiek loved her more than ever. He loved her matter-of-fact courage. The surgeon decided to operate and excise the pre-cancerous cells. She (it was a she) proposed to enter by making an incision along the edge of the areola, so the scar would be almost invisible. 'I'm lucky to have a woman,' Véra said. 'A man might have taken the whole thing off.'

She had divined an actual affair between Rysiek and Jadwiga – since his sudden, then extended, silence on the subject of his dentist, after weeks of garrulous agonising. Now her remarks about the male sex, the sex in general, were spiked with a new tartness. That was how Rysiek knew she knew.

They entered a yet further stage: at first, they had adopted a discreet, a disguised voice; then his interest was out in the open but technically innocent; now they spoke under cover of darkness like enemies pretending friendship. Words weren't weapons. They were warnings, threats, diplomatic double-speak, primed with wariness.

Her conversation had an habitual ironic edge. But she was calm. And sexually confident enough to wait for the infatuation to wear itself out. She knew that Rysiek cared about her and she thought that was more important than love, more durable than passion. She had cared about him, cared for him, for almost as long as she could remember – ever since she was that grave girl who accepted his proposal unsmiling, knowing that love would have to last a long time.

Two months after Véra left the hospital, Rysiek was cleaning his teeth and she was in the shower. He stopped, moved by the tiny blue scar left by the draining tube inserted after the operation. It was virtually invisible except in water. It wasn't a scar, it was a speck – and it held his heart. Seeing it, he found it hard to breathe.

The left breast was smaller than the other now. But the entry scar – about two inches long – was well disguised by the areola. As promised by the surgeon. She had done a good job. And a course of Tamoxifen was dealing with the cancer chemically.

As he stared at the blue scar, Rysiek decided to confess to Véra and break off the affair with Jadwiga. Not now. When she was feeling better.

And he did confess, but he wasn't able to break off the affair with Jadwiga, as the incident with the thong later proved – to Véra's undisguised contempt – as it fell from his jeans.

Véra might have been even angrier had she known that the thong was an item from Agnieszka's wardrobe. Jadwiga's taste in underwear was surprisingly demure. Sensible. Black and white. It didn't run to thongs. Whereas Agnieszka had little else.

Rysiek had been rushing for the train back to Lublin and dressed in a hurry, while Agnieszka lay back on her pillows, looking over her spectacles, laughing at her uxorious lover.

How did it happen?

How did it happen that a man who had fallen in love with his wife again was now fucking three people at once?

Well, for a start, he was only fucking one person – Agnieszka. And not that often because she was in Warsaw and he lived in Lublin.

Véra he loved, but she was uninterested in sex at the moment. The regime of Tamoxifen left her nauseated and sexually indifferent – and she was expected to take it for at least two years, while the cancer was monitored with regular mammograms.

And Jadwiga?

Rysiek tried to break it off. He could still feel the weight of the coffee spoon between his index and his middle finger as he brought his gaze up from her table top – to meet her brown eyes and hear his lips slowly say that 'This has got to stop.'

'Because of Véra's cancer?'

'Yes. No: it's more complicated than that. But, basically, yes. I can't do this to her. Not now.'

He couldn't explain about the blue speck. He didn't want to wound her.

'No,' she said, 'I understand.'

And it was her understanding that made the break-up quite impossible. She was on Véra's side. She really felt for her. Jadwiga was completely genuine and completely without calculation.

'We have to stop,' she said. 'I can see that. It's the only decent thing to do.'

A great tear bulged in her eye and sped down her nose. 'Only it will break my heart.'

So he couldn't leave her. He loved her. He loved Véra and he loved Jadwiga, too.

And he slept with neither.

Somehow, from this moment, it evolved between Jadwiga and Rysiek that they met, as usual, talked, cuddled, kissed, but never took off their clothes. It was an unspoken compromise, a concession to what they both felt about Véra. Their *affaire blanche* was an act of solidarity with the afflicted flesh of Véra. And it equalled Rysiek's de facto *mariage blanc* with Véra and Véra's cancer.

———

The *mariage blanc* is more common than we think. I have known two. Sometimes it arrives gradually. Sometimes the marriage is like that from the start.

155

Of course, it is a cliché that all marriages are opaque, because they are. So how does one discover that a couple have a *mariage blanc* when they behave as if their sex life is a going concern?

The woman in the marriage tells you. It is never the man. Because the man is the problem. He spends too much time late at night in his study, doing essential accounts, reading up on an interest, pursuing research. And the woman wonders how they got out of the habit. And whether there was something wrong in the first place.

She tries to remember what their sex was like. Was it satisfactory? She'd thought so at the time, though it had never been urgent or often. It was like the weekly shop.

And the woman blames herself.

She goes to the library, she goes on the internet. She tells someone.

But there are no answers to a man's indifference. Indifference is an enigma – the Bartleby in some men that would simply prefer not.

Companionship might be a compensation, but, without intimacy, with taboo areas for discussion, it is mere cohabitation. Not peaceful coexistence but irritated coexistence. And the woman confides in someone else, usually another woman. She wants to know how unusual her existence is.

Sometimes, there is no sex right from the beginning. No sex before marriage either. The husband is sexually active, but only with himself. He masturbates. It has always been this way. Asked casually, an old 'girlfriend' reports that their sex consisted of him jerking off while he watched her naked from the other side of the room. 'Nothing to be jealous of.' The wife tells someone else, a man this time – a man who becomes her lover.

And Piotr? Just now Piotr was in a *mariage blanc*. But we know why that was. He was depressed. His cock was depressed. He didn't feel up to it.

He wrote a one-line poem called 'Sex'.

'We wake up with the remote between us.'

———

But *Agnieszka*?

She and Rysiek had several meetings, in Warsaw and Lublin, to discuss the typeface, the jacket design, the weight of paper – more meetings, Véra felt, than were strictly necessary.

'Look out for her. That one is trouble, Rysiek.' She had read Agnieszka's typescript.

'I like her, actually,' Rysiek said.

'I know you do.'

Véra looked at him.

'Watch.' She squeezed her teabag against the side of her mug, squashed it with her teaspoon. 'Like a cockroach.'

'I'll be careful.'

'You'd better be.'

Their sixth meeting was in a Lublin bar. They ordered half a bottle of Danziger Goldwasser and a plate of zakuski. Rysiek could tell that Agnieszka thought he was attractive. The signs were obvious. She laughed. He could see her wet teeth, the squeezed light in her eyes. She leaned into his personal space. Tonight she was wearing her tits. They brushed him a couple of times. They shook when she laughed. Rysiek watched her work her skirt down over her long legs before she went to the toilet. It had ridden high in her low seat. Only the table between them had stopped him seeing the gusset of her tights.

Rysiek was worried – attracted, but worried. And tipsy. 'I'll walk you to the station.' And he helped her into her coat, watched her long fingers find the sleeve.

In the fan-tailed street he felt safer.

She took his arm when she stumbled. Her body warmth, the heat from her face, whelmed against him.

'Would you like to fuck me? Why don't you ask me if I'll fuck you?'

Rysiek's solution was frankness. 'Because I'm married and I already have a girlfriend.'

'No problem. That's fine by me. I have a boyfriend, too.'

They walked, arm in arm, in silence, for a hundred yards. He didn't know what to say. But as they walked, the silence seemed a solution in itself.

Until Agnieszka spoke. 'I have a shaved fanny. Don't you want to see it? You might want to fuck it with your lovely stiff cock.'

He did.

He took her to the flat on the seventeenth floor where they had their printing press. He fucked her on the floor beside the paper-making tank. Her fanny wasn't shaved.

'It will be. Don't worry,' she said.

And it was.

––––––––

Why? Why was she interested in this older man? She cared about her poetry. She liked Rysiek, but she cared about her poetry. She wanted a handsome book, something handsomely produced, which is why she had approached Rysiek in the first place. She preferred never to leave anything to chance. At university, she fucked both of her tutors – well, the two who would be writing her references. One of them 'helped' her to write the thesis component. (On dystopias in Margaret Atwood, Huxley, Karp, Lem, Zamyatin and Orwell.) She wasn't cynically seeking favours. She saw herself as rewarding favours, sex as gratitude.

And Rysiek was good in bed. Or good beside the paper-tank.

Moreover, she didn't have a boyfriend right now.

––––––––

'Agnieszka was still a great fuck. A great fuck.' Piotr's verdict, you'll remember, when he resumed his affair with Agnieszka.

But did Agnieszka think that she was a great fuck? She was certainly expert and proficient. Another girl had taught her to kiss at school. They practised for hours. She kissed to a very high standard, grasping the theory of tongues, realising that the tongue tight in the mouth was a simile for a cock tight in a cunt. (So she didn't get the perverse pleasure of the loose lips, the drool of aftermath, of slack exhaustion, the emblem of having been fucked.)

When she sucked a man off, she always did it facing him, so he could see his cock in her mouth. She always swallowed the semen. She was efficient, highly trained, experienced, an athlete. She had no objection to dildos. She had no objection to being sodomised, provided there was KY and her anal sphincter was relaxed. Penetration was easier post-orgasm.

But she thought she had a weakness.

———

In my first week in Oxford as an undergraduate, I went to a bop in the Wheatsheaf, which was down an alley off the High Street. The protocol was that you danced a couple of dances, then took the girl into the alley – where you kissed her, if she agreed to go outside.

I remember the girl I picked up. She was older than me, good-looking, maybe a fraction taller, with substantial breasts I was hoping to feel.

When I kissed her, I mustered all my expertise.

I was mortified, therefore, when she said, as the kiss was completed: 'So, you're a freshman, then.'

'How do you know?' I asked, steeling myself for the worst.

'Your clothes. New sweater, new trousers, new shoes. All the second years are scruffs.'

———

I saw a van covered in dirt, in which was written: 'I bet you wish your wife was as dirty as this.'

For the sadist, the swallowing of semen, or hard fucking of the mouth, is exciting because it is done against the wishes, the erotic preference, of the woman. Acquiescence is therefore a declaration of love. It might also speak to the masochism of the partner. For whom forced compliance is better than easy acquiescence.

Philip Roth's early fiction argues that the swallowing of semen is a crucial aspect of sex. But Roth doesn't understand obscenity, perversity: which is that something unpleasant is embraced because it is unpleasant. (Just as long as it isn't too unpleasant.) Roth doesn't understand that the woman who *welcomed* semen swallowing, being fucked hard in the mouth, would not gratify him because she would not be overcoming her resistance. Nor would he be overcoming her resistance.

And, lastly, he doesn't realise that automatic acquiescence would get boring. His early fiction demonstrates only a rudimentary grasp of crop rotation. It is obsessed with oats.

Agnieszka would have suited him perfectly – for a time. Then he would have felt the chill of her clean efficiency. It was difficult to violate her technique.

———

But that wasn't what she thought her weakness was.

She took a long time to come, even with the aid of ventilated fantasies. In a way, this meant she had no sexual confidence, only a solid technique, sexual competence. She hardly ever faked an orgasm. It was a point of honour. She liked to come. She was capable of coming twice. But sometimes she avoided sex if she felt her excitement levels were low: because the sex was good the day before; because she didn't want a marathon.

She didn't like to disappoint herself.

Ideally, she liked her nipple sucked, sucked hard, so that it tingled all the next day. Then her orgasm was intense.

Agnieszka never realised that a lover might not mind, might even welcome, these extended bouts of sexual excitement, might prefer the increased intensity of his release after forty minutes or an hour of aching arousal.

Poor Piotr certainly preferred it. For him, it wasn't delay, but deliberately chosen, perverse deferral. It was one of the reasons why he had loved her.

It wasn't a weakness, but she saw it as a weakness. So it was a weakness.

She considered her sex life as emblematic, central and somehow wanting. It wasn't the art of surfeit. She could sense her boundaries. And superstitiously she knew her poetry and her sexual life were symbiotic.

She knew she was good, but she knew she wasn't a genius.

———

Jadwiga was the genius. A natural. Despite her sensible knickers.

Agnieszka sensed this, without knowing anything about her. Rysiek was completely discreet. He had a 'girlfriend' and there the information stopped. Agnieszka managed to be jealous of her rival even though Jadwiga and Rysiek hadn't fucked for months.

And she was right to be jealous.

Véra apparently made a good recovery. The histology was good. Tamoxifen controlled the pre-cancerous cells and when, after a time, it was found to carry an increased risk of uterine cancer and clots, another medication replaced it. First Arimidex, then Raloxifene. She was certain, although she knew Rysiek still saw Jadwiga, that their sexual relationship was over. She could trust his love. She felt secure. And she believed him when he told her he and Jadwiga were friendly celibates.

So she was devastated when the thong fell from his jeans. He couldn't tell her that it belonged to someone else.

It was as if she could taste the acrid taste of all the chemicals she'd ever taken.

'That expression, Rysiek. You know, "It leaves a nasty taste in your mouth." It's absolutely accurate. You've lied to me and I've believed you all this time. Do you know what it feels like to be lied to, to be lied to systematically? Of course you don't. You only know what it's like to lie, you liar. I'm getting a divorce.'

A divorce for one thong? For one black thong, even if lightly soiled with a white smear at its thinnest part?

If he hadn't loved her so openly, so obviously, Véra wouldn't have minded so much. But she felt, for the first time in a couple of years, that it was all right to trust him. She believed that he loved her. And we know she was right.

But, of course, there was another reason that made the thong unbearable – the crucial flake of snow, the shout, which started this avalanche that was to carry away their marriage.

Véra had another outbreak of cancer, probably caused by taking Tamoxifen, even though her physician had reorganised her medication. It wasn't uterine cancer – sometimes a side effect of Tamoxifen – but cancer of the vulva. Just as Véra was thinking they might resume sexual relations.

In fact, one night they tried. She was excited and wet but penetration was uncomfortable. 'We're out of practice,' she whispered. 'I don't know how long it's been exactly. How long *has* it been, actually?'

Rysiek adopted the voice of an old crone: 'Sixty year come Michaelmas.'

'At *least*,' he added in his normal voice. 'That's all right, Vérochka,' he said. 'Slowly gradually. Slowly gradually.'

Then he laughed again, as he put on the tremulous soprano of Vivien Leigh in *Gone with the Wind*: 'Be gentle with me, my darling, please be gentle with your little girl.'

Véra laughed, too. And they turned aside to sleep. By the bedside, the rim of a white china pot of Earl Grey tea glowed in the dark, making the most of the light from an elliptical moon.

In the morning, just near the entrance, she found a lump the size of a marble on the right wall of her vagina. Her doctors thought it might be a recurrence of a Bartholin cyst from ten years previously. However, the histology confirmed it was an aggressive cancer.

'A very, very rare condition,' the consultant said, more to Rysiek than to Véra. 'Perhaps 800 cases a year. In Poland. So, rare. Very rare. And the majority of cases occur in women in their seventies and eighties. Where it's a type of skin cancer – generally slow growing.'

'What is the recommended procedure in *rare* cases like this?' Véra was angry. She wanted to tell the consultant that she was the patient. She kept the anger out of her voice, but the irony was audible. For her, the rarity of her condition couldn't have mattered less. 'Is there a recommended procedure, in fact?'

The consultant oncologist plucked the white handkerchief from his breast pocket, patted his neck twice and rearranged the linen folds. He was upset, too, and he felt emotion was unprofessional.

She would need two surgeons – a consultant gynaecologist to remove the tumour, and consultant reconstructive plastic surgeon (a burns specialist) to reconstruct her vagina. The operation would take five to six hours. The tumour would be removed, as well as both lymph nodes and lymph glands in the groin, and the tissue surrounding the tumour. By then Véra would have lost a third of her vagina.

Then the operation would be continued by the reconstructive burns specialist. He would fill the hole left by the consultant surgeon gynaecologist – by cutting a portion of tissue (15 cm long and 5 cm wide) from the fold under Véra's right buttock. The tissue – selected to contain a blood vessel and an artery – would be lifted up on three sides, rotated through 180 degrees, then turned inside into the vagina and sutured into place. Eventually, nerves would grow there.

Three days before she was due to go into hospital, the thong fell out of Rysiek's jeans.

He had only gone to Warsaw to stop Agnieszka from coming to Lublin to 'look after' him when Véra was in hospital. Of course, Agnieszka would not have offered had Rysiek explained the nature of the surgical procedure. But he couldn't. It was too intimate. He felt it would be betraying Véra more intimately than if he slept with Agnieszka. He felt as if he would be conferring an advantage on the other woman. Naturally, then, Agnieszka felt this was a lovers' opportunity, not to be squandered. Her persistence was only to be expected. She was not to blame.

Had he told her the truth, she would have kept away.

Rysiek wasn't to know Agnieszka had a cancer phobia. Fear of contagion would have kept her silent in Warsaw. But he knew hardly anything about her, except the ways she was in bed.

Strangely, Rysiek distinguished between Agnieszka and Jadwiga. He told Jadwiga the truth, without feeling Véra was at all betrayed.

Véra refused to let him visit her in hospital. For her, Rysiek was secondary – to be ignored. And he was a secondary – to be defeated. 'I need to concentrate on getting better. I haven't the time to think about you. I don't want to have to think about you. I don't want to listen to you. I don't care if you're sorry. I am going to get well again. I will not be beaten.'

And she wasn't. She got well again.

It was a bitter legal action. She wanted to deprive him of everything she could. Her lawyer was a woman who had been divorced herself. Top lawyers don't have personal lives. There isn't time to make a career and live a life. The legal profession under the age of 40 is fucked – if they're any good. And this one was a brilliant advocate.

He lost the palace he had so meticulously restored. With its rare Faïence stove and the stone fireplace he bought in Albi. He moved into the other flat at first but it was like living in a car. Or under a car – there was so much machinery.

Eventually, he moved in with Jadwiga and broke it off with Agnieszka – which wasn't easy and involved him in some queasy, awkward sexual overlap. In the end, though, he would have broken her fingers to loosen her grip. When Agnieszka realised how much he hated her, she walked away.

'You can't blame your life on me, Rysiek.'

'I know, I know it's not your fault,' he said.

He was trying to be reasonable. But he blamed her for everything.

Especially the divorce, which had destroyed the love he felt for Véra.

A thing he would have thought impossible.

All the reviews of Agnieszka's Harlan and Harlan chapbook, *The Cost of Meat*, were restrained about the personal material in the sequence. Some mentioned its customary candour, commiserated with the male subject, but several called in question the very idea of life feeding art. One reviewer recalled a visiting senior English poet who had denied that his poems were about adultery, pointing out their literary ancestry in the venerable tradition of *amour courtois*. The reviewer located *The Cost of Meat* in another tradition: erotic *flyteing*. Other reviewers – mostly men, it has to be said – praised Agnieszka's imagery, her mastery of tone and rhythm, and completely ignored the flaying of Marsyas at the heart of the sequence.

Piotr might have taken comfort from this reception.

But he was too afraid to read any of the reviews. Or to discuss the book with anyone.

Agnieszka had asked for a copy to be sent. It bore no inscription. But he knew whom it came from. He thought she should have called it *Friendly Fire*. It was a better title. He was right.

———

Colette Clark, daughter of Sir Kenneth Clark, famous friend/assistant of Margot Fonteyn, was spending a weekend at Glyndebourne with the Christies. Rex asked Mary Christie where George was. He was in one of the outhouses, plucking pheasants he'd shot a fortnight before. Rex went out to say hello. George was in his wellies and Barbour, plucking diligently and listening to a portable radio. 'Oh fuck off,' he said. 'Sacred hour. I'm trying to listen to *The Archers* omnibus.'

An hour later, lunch was ready, but no sign of George. They started the soup without him and were halfway through some delicious pasta, served with a rocket salad from the garden, when George finally made his entrance. 'Sorry,' he said. 'Sacred *Archers* hour. Didn't mean to be rude.' Gripping the soup bowl with both hands, he raised it to his mouth, stopped, laughed, put down the soup bowl and held out the index finger on his right hand. 'Smells exactly like an arsehole.'

'*George!*' said Colette.

'Promise you,' he said. 'Have a sniff.'

'GEORGE!'

In the old auditorium at Glyndebourne, usually, but not inevitably, two days after heavy rain, you could sometimes smell the 'drains' – a euphemism for the dog's breath of stale sewage.

When Glyndebourne was rebuilt, the acoustic improved and so did the unpredictable banausic reek of old farts from the ancient septic tank. But one thing remained the same: the particular intense pong in all the ladies' lavatories – not of farts, naturally, but of asparagus.

Ian McEwan's early story 'Reflections of a Kept Ape' is narrated by an ape in the manner of Henry James. 'Eaters of asparagus know the scent it lends the urine,' it begins.

But only *some* eaters of asparagus know the scent it lends the urine. In fact, only one in four people has the required enzyme. My information comes from Richard Dawkins, the zoologist.

It shows, too, that one should never assume that one's experience is automatically shared by other human beings – an objection often levelled at me by my friend, the philosopher Galen Strawson.

On the other hand, everyone knows what an arsehole smells like. *Sulphur dung of lions.* And I should risk saying that this is a smell we fundamentally like, though we are socially conditioned to deny it. Non-smokers often say, correctly, that smokers' breath smells of shit. Cigars are undisguisedly faecal. The verdict of non-smokers may not be the crushing negative intended. Can it be that, at some deep level, we like the smell of shit?

Of course not. Ridiculous.

Not even the smell of your own shit?

Literature is implicitly predicated on this assumption of fundamental identity, as Ian McEwan maintained in his 2001 Richard Hillary Memorial Lecture, in which he used Darwin's *The Expression of the Emotions in Man and Animals* to show the shared, unalterable reservoir of human emotions.

At the same time, great writers can make us experience entirely foreign experiences – cowardice and bravery under fire in, say, Tolstoy's *Sebastopol Sketches* or sexual masochism in McEwan's 'Pornography' – a story in which the hero's penis is aroused by the thought of its imminent amputation. George Eliot believed that the moral function of literature was to widen the range of our sympathies.

Henry James, in a justifiably cross letter to H. G. Wells (who had mocked him in *Boon*), wrote: 'It is when that history and curiosity have been determined in a way most different from my own that I myself want to get at them – precisely *for* the extension of life, which is the novel's best gift.'

Henry James and penile amputation as an extension of life.

There is a risk here for the writer that is impossible to underwrite. Two risks, actually, depending on whether we are imagining or transcribing experience. In both instances, the writer can only consult himself. What would I do in this situation? What did I do in this situation?

There is always the risk of assuming a common identity where there is only solipsism. This is the theme of subjectivity. Readers do not recognise what you take to be commonplace. Sometimes, of course, they are only pretending not to recognise what is unacceptable.

The other risk is more complicated. The writer imagines something outside the pale. He enters the mind of a serial killer, say. His job is not to recoil but to empathise, to inhabit the bizarre psychic landscape. The writer *assumes* moral disapproval – of Bill Sikes, of Regan and Goneril, of Browning's cruel Duke of Ferrara in 'My Last Duchess' – but it is taken for granted, it has to be implicit, if it is not to be hectoring. And great art will always transcend narrow moral judgement and find itself in the quiddity of character in *this* time and place. That glowing, incandescent cinder of bloodied hair that flies up the chimney when Sikes tries to burn the murder weapon. Denunciation is best left to the Archbishop of Canterbury. It has no place in art.

We like being punitive: public executions, burnings and beheadings, weren't an historical aberration. Righteous cruelty is in our nature.

And this is further complicated by the *bien-pensant* convictions of readers – some of which are inevitably outraged by good art because it deals with what *is* the case, not with what *ought* to be the case.

For example, we know that children are sexually innocent. But, in *Giving Offense* (1996), Coetzee observed, calmly, irrefutably, that the idea of children's sexual innocence is a construct imposed by society: 'we have all been children and know – unless we prefer to forget – how little innocent we were.'

It follows that good writing is bound to give offence – by saying inconveniently unconventional things, by disagreeing. And therefore will often seem disagreeable.

———

On the *Today* programme (BBC Radio 4, 21 May 2002) Professor Merkin at the University of Missouri, Kansas, was interviewed. He had written that, in some cultures, there are sexual relations between adults and children. He argued (like Coetzee) that children have sexuality and this is being denied by society just as the Victorians denied female sexuality. Right-wing Christian groups were demanding he should be sacked from his state-funded post. University authorities were asserting his right to intellectual enquiry.

The merkin is a pubic wig, originally worn by prostitutes who had shaved their genitals to get rid of pubic lice. The pubic wig is now worn by people without pubic hair (for whatever reason) and by 'nude' performers who wish to conceal the detail of their genitals. In *Lolita*, Humbert Humbert refers to a mature sexual partner, his first wife, Valeria, as 'an animated merkin': this is a metaphor. Humbert and Nabokov, both Europeans, mean she is a *substitute* – for the nymphet he would prefer.

Why 'both Europeans'? Because some Americans used not to know what the word 'merkin' meant. There is a former *New Yorker* film critic called Daphne Merkin, who wrote in the magazine about her erotic obsession with being spanked. There is a Merkin Theater and a Merkin Concert Hall at 129 West 67th Street. There again, in American, 'fanny' means 'backside'. In English, 'fanny' means the yo-yo between a woman's legs.

(Especially if she is using a tampon.)

Is it a calling, a vocation, merkin-making? Like the priesthood? Like pedagogy? Like chiropody?

Or is it just a craft? And what degree of craft? One size fits all, off-the-peg or bespoke?

Are there merkin sweatshops in the garment districts of big cities? Can it be a full-time occupation? Is it seasonal work? What are the retail outlets? Or is it all mail order?

Is it universal? Or is it specialist, a minority affair? We are back to the critical question.

Actually, it is, of course, a specialism within a more familiar service industry. Among the massed instruments for masking baldness – full wigs, toupees, hair transplants, extensions – it is the humble triangle.

There was a small item in Tina Brown's *Vanity Fair* about Hollywood dinner parties and how boring they were – because all everyone talked about was who'd had plastic surgery and who had big cocks. Supermarket outlets were outraged and Tina had to tour selected Wal-Marts to calm the buyers.

In 2001 there was a scandal at the Tarpaulin Health Club in Manhattan, when certain members took to twitching away the towels of other members to reveal their members and ridicule their rigs. Legal action was threatened in at least one instance.

Piotr recovered his sexual self-confidence only when he went to bed with Agnieszka again, after Rysiek was divorced by Véra, and had decided to drop Agnieszka and marry Jadwiga.

It was five years after the publication of *The Cost of Meat*. If anything, Piotr was the more highly regarded poet, though neither was famous.

They were both older. Piotr's eyebrows were permanently surprised. He approached her at a party with a glass of wine in his hand. 'Aren't you the notorious Agnieszka Dotrowicz?'

'The same.'

'What happened to Nana Mouskouri? The signature spectacles?'

'Contact lenses.'

'I thought you should have called your book *Friendly Fire*.'

'Definitely a better title.'

They looked at each other, unsmiling. Piotr raised his glass to her and walked away.

Three hours later Agnieszka was drunk. Piotr was sitting on a sofa talking to a 25-year-old girl, trying to make himself heard above the music. Agnieszka made her way through the crowd and stood over him, swaying. In no hurry, he finished what he was saying before he looked up.

Agnieszka didn't speak. She mouthed, Take me home.

Piotr shook his head twice.

She mouthed, Please.

He shook his head quite slowly once more.

Agnieszka tried to mouth something else, but her lips were locked. She tried to mime the word again, but couldn't continue. Her stiff lips stopped. It was as if she were coming. She moved her head from side to side. Big tears, the tears of a child, sorrow unconfined and uncontainable, a rupture of sacs, sachets of salt water, slipping and spilling and bursting.

She bit her handkerchief and shook. He took her home to her apartment.

In bed, the next morning, she said she had once seen a gecko in Venice, on the marble floor of a rented two-room apartment. It was barely an inch long. An eddy, a sway, a sashay on the floor. It moved like a belly dancer.

'It was exquisite. I caught it in a glass tumbler. But I was nervous. And I cut off a fraction of leg with the edge of the glass. I have never forgiven myself.'

(Basia and the three boys were in Wladiswałała on a camping trip.)

————

There is a letter written by James Joyce to his wife, Nora, about the size of his cock. 'You stuck my prick into your cunt and began to ride me up and down. Perhaps the horn I had was not big enough for you for I remember that you bent down to my face and murmured tenderly "Fuck up, love! Fuck up, love!"' (3 December 1909.)

On the other hand, Bloom in the bath sees 'the limp father of thousands, a languid floating flower' – limp perhaps, but more length to it.

On 26 October 2008 the *Observer* published a special magazine supplement on sex. It included the results of a questionnaire. No introductory overall information about the questionnaire or the respondents was given. To the question

'Are you happy with the size of your penis?', 86 per cent answered 'yes' and 14 per cent answered 'no'.

Since there's nothing to be done about it, it is as well to be 'happy' about it. Or contented. Or resigned. Not a lot of choice, actually, you might say.

Unless. This is a selection of the subject lines for penis enlargement emails on 24 June 2003. Recently, these spams have been filtered out. I do not imagine, however, that the widespread anxiety they address and exploit has diminished.

> Effort and Expense of Having a Large, Manly Penis! eat
> Penis Enlargement / Lengthening Secrets Now Revealed
>   onotlesxkytr
> Increased Penis Strength j hcq uqq l
> Enlarge Your Penis Guaranteed
> Safely Feel Young
> Size DOES Matter! Enlarge Your Penis Now!
> MALE LIBIDO
> Achieve ROCK HARD erections any time you want. s
> 'Penis enlargement that works'
> 100% effective penis enlargement
> Bigger P@*is head – created a more mushroomed &
>   muscular look

Everyone is insecure. How could it be otherwise when those arias of emotion and excitement depend on such laughably primitive mechanisms, large, small or medium? Sex isn't simply subjective. It is complete solipsism.

Sexuality and insecurity are inseparable. Excitement is inseparable from danger. 'The awful daring of a moment's surrender.' Eliot's line captures the paradox at the heart of sexuality: the courage of fear.

The 'daring', the bravery, serves not conquest but 'surrender'.

No one is perfect, so no one is completely confident. In *The Female Eunuch*, Germaine Greer speaks for us all, men and women, when she writes that 'No woman wants to find out she has a twat like a horse-collar.' Barbra Streisand in a 1966 interview on *Late Night Line Up* said: 'I have both feelings. I have a confidence in myself also with a deep insecurity. The insecurity feeds the confidence and the confidence nurtures the insecurity and they work hand in hand.' You would imagine that the insecurity undermined the confidence, while the confidence countered the insecurity. Obviously, Streisand is no Aristotle.

But it is clear that confidence and insecurity coexist in everyone. More, this mimics the erectile function in the male – with the nitric oxide prompting expansion and another enzyme countering the nitric oxide. *Das Ding an sich*, the cock, is cocky and self-deflationary.

On President Kennedy's 45th birthday, the 36-year-old Marilyn Monroe was introduced by Peter Lawford as 'pulchritudinous and punctual', then finally, after two further comic introductions and delays, as 'the late Marilyn Monroe'.

She materialises like ectoplasm. She is spotlit but seems a source of light. An isotope. Her dress has been sewn on so tight she has to hurry her ankles – quick as the fly-wheel of a watch – barely able to keep up. She twinkles across on a tightrope and reaches the safety of the podium. The late Marilyn Monroe.

She flicks the microphone with her finger. Grasps it in her fist. Runs her other hand along its length. Sighs on to it. And finally sings into it with that inimitable husky hesitant whisper and her high exaggerated vibrato. It is part Marlene

Dietrich, part female impersonator. It sends up sex and manages to be completely sexy.

Happy birthday, Mr President.

JFK thanks her for that 'wholesome' rendition.

The universally desired, late Marilyn Monroe suffered from endometriosis, a disease of the pelvis, caused by the migration of uterine tissue to organs outside the uterus – where it irritates the nerve endings of the bladder, the bowels and the fallopian tubes, and causes inflammation, scarring, fibrous adhesions and infertility. In 1961 Marilyn Monroe had her sixth gynaecological operation. She suffered at least two miscarriages, three marriages and numerous affairs. She was insecure. Of course she was insecure. She died of it – of insecurity poisoning.

———

The *Sunday Times* 'Style' section (29 September 2002) ran a piece about how lucky Francesca Annis was to be living with, as she then was, Ralph Fiennes, a man eighteen years her younger. 'He is also one of the world's hottest sex symbols. In fact, according to the director of his latest film, *Red Dragon*, he insisted on a nude scene and proved to be so well endowed that they had to digitally remove several inches.'

Now, why would that be? Supposing you were a director who wanted to sell your movie: you might want to trail the nude scene. But you protect your star from the charge of looking, well, average, by claiming to have removed 'several' inches by digital technology. I think the director was being economical with the truth.

On the other hand, I met Ralph in the River Café. It must have been in the autumn of 2001. He said he wanted to do a performance of Christopher Logue's *All Day Permanent Red*, which he had read in *Areté*. I said I'd just seen the Verse Theater Manhattan's all-female version of Logue's *War Music*.

Ralph was dismissive, confident. 'No good. That poetry needs cock. Tell him [Logue] I've got lots of cock.'

Some of it on the cutting floor. I believe this, too. There was no call for him to lie.

I believe in Piotr before and after. Dauntless and daunted. Daunted and dauntless.

————

Rysiek died in a car accident, two days after his marriage to Jadwiga, when a Mercedes travelling in the opposite direction crossed the central reservation. A cover of Leonard Cohen's 'Alleluia!' by Rufus Wainwright had just come on the car radio and Rysiek put out his right hand to increase the volume on the new Blaupunkt (a wedding present to himself). The collision took the Trabant into the path of an empty car transporter going at speed down the middle lane. He died from multiple injuries, especially a broken spine. He was 59.

The other driver was also killed.

They never discovered the cause of the accident. It seemed an act of God. In fact, it was a bee in the other car – a beautiful black bee with a red arse, like the end of a cigar in mid-air. It never stung the driver of the blue Mercedes. It didn't need to. He was allergic to bee-stings, as he knew to his cost – and as Rysiek now also knew to *his* cost.

The bee crawled out of the wreckage like King Kong miniaturised and flew away with the usual difficulty, unwieldy, unlikely as a tilted helicopter taking off.

———

If you are about to have a heart attack, one of the symptoms is the desire to defecate. This is why it is sometimes thought that the act of straining at stool causes the heart failure.

When my former colleague Tony Nuttall was writing the Lord Northcliffe Lectures for University College, London, he consulted me about a point of decorum. Would it be all right, he wanted to know, if, in a discussion of the Aristotelian concept of *katharsis*, or purgation, he said that perhaps the analogy Aristotle had in mind was one of those violent expulsions of a hard turd? I advised him that it would be all right.

Tony died on 24 January 2007 of an unexpected heart attack at the early age of 69. He had just finished a book on Shakespeare, *Shakespeare the Thinker*, and it was about to be published to some of the best reviews he ever received. But he died in New College just before publication – on the lavatory. Like Evelyn Waugh. Like Arius, the 'illstarred heresiarch' in *Ulysses* 'with clotted hinderparts'. Like Francis Bacon's lover George Dyer. Like Elvis. Like Vespasian, who is cited when brother Bobby dies in *Tristram Shandy* – one of Tony's favourite books. 'Vespasian died in a jest upon his close-stool.'

———

When Véra politely snubbed her at Rysiek's funeral, Jadwiga was surprised and hurt. But of course, she knew nothing about the thong. Rysiek hadn't told her. He couldn't tell her. Obviously.

Véra's veil lent her features a silk-screen vagueness. But her laconic greeting left no room for ambiguity. Nor did her out-stretched gloved hand encourage an embrace. There was to be no solidarity of grief. She didn't wish Rysiek back, and she wanted no one else. She had had enough. Her mother's iguana neck held sway.

So, in spite of her new vagina, Véra found her virginity, at 61, as it were.

Both women were a little surprised to see Agnieszka crying so readily. But they put it down to poetry – an art they thought of as essentially lachrymose. (Neither remembered *The Cost of Meat* and its dry-eyed detail. Neither understood anything about poetry.) Agnieszka was naturally sentimental. Her poetry wasn't. And she was crying because she remembered how much Rysiek had hated her in the end. Her tears were for herself.

It was a perfect cloudless August day, so it was much too hot. The cemetery was like an artist's studio, crowded with plinths, a vernissage of cynical sculpture. It was the retrospec-tive, tongue in chic, of some academician, worshipped by the rabble.

In the evening, there was a hailstorm.

Oxford – Areté – Venezia, 2001–8

Acknowledgements

I am very grateful to Alan Ryan, Richard Dawkins, Nicolas Slater, Alison Macdonald, Nina Raine, Patrick Hunter. Agnieszka Deputowska checked my Polish spelling.

And thanks, of course, to Milan Kundera, who invented this kind of novel. A last 'digression'. In February 2007 I gave my French French colleague at New College, Frédérique Aït-Touati, a copy of 'I Remember My Mother Dying', a poem of mine which was published in the *Times Literary Supplement* in 2005. It reminded her of Georges Perec's *Je me souviens* (1978). Had I read it? I explained that Perec's brilliant book was twice indebted – to Harry Mathews, and to Joe Brainard. Mathews, the only foreign member of Oulipo, had shown Perec *I Remember* (1970), *I Remember More* (1971) and *More I Remember More* (1973) by Joe Brainard, the inventor of the technique. As Perec acknowledges: 'Le titre, la forme et, dans une certaine mesure, l'esprit de ces textes s'inspirent des *I Remember* de Joe Brainard.'

I have no idea who translated *Pnin* into Polish. Obviously that distinguished person bears no resemblance at all to my character Piotr. I just prefer my details to be specific.

Most people know the Peter Brook anecdote which Olga and the playwright share. For those who don't, it is said that Brook was directing a play with Gielgud in the lead. Rehearsals consisted of exercises and improvisations. One morning Brook asked the cast to come into the rehearsal and do something that would 'terrify' him. Gielgud said, 'We open in two weeks.'

Donna Poppy copy-edited the book with her customary genius.

My readers know who they are. My love and thanks to them.